CHAPTER 1

THE EMBERS.

"They had obviously discovered the consolations of alcohol and cynicism late in life."

--Kurt Vonnegut Jr., _The Sirens of Titan_ 1959

"Did I tell you I used to be a spy?" the man sitting at the end of the bar was chatting up a woman with bottle blond hair wearing tight red jeans. Both of them looked pretty close to their sell by date.

"No- you did not" She answered but did not turn his way. She stared straight ahead into the mirror behind the bar.

"I was, I was a double naught spy and I drove a fancy sports car, an Aston-Martin DB7" the man at the end of the bar had shoe polish dyed black hair and his shirt was open far too many buttons down from the collar exposing a gold chain and too much chest hair.

"Uh uh" the bleached blond woman was losing interest.

"I've been to France, Belgium, Poland, Morocco, Lichtenstein- all over" the man at the end of the bar had some difficulty with the word "Lichtenstein".

"I have never been east of Lynn" the woman replied, staring straight ahead at her reflection.

"I would love to take you to Europe sometime"

"I don't even know you, why would I go?"

"Don't you feel a connection?" the man at the corner of the bar slid a little closer to the bleached blond woman.

The woman stared at him for a few seconds and squinted like she was trying to get him in focus. "With you? No, I actually don't. I need to get something out of my car" The woman got up and walked toward the door. The man at the bar did not notice she took a detour into the ladies' room.

It was a dark and stormy night. Well, maybe not, it was a rum and Coke night and last call at The Embers. Tony stood up from his bar stool at the corner of the bar and for a few seconds felt like he had just gotten off the tilt-a-whirl at Nantasket. He thought about the Buick parked out back, his trailer and the woman who an hour ago left to "get something out of her car". He decided that it may be best that the Buick stays out back and that he walks the two or so miles back to the park. It was summer, and the night cooled off the heat of the day, so a walk would be pleasant and have fewer legal ramifications. He paid his tab and grabbed a handful of little pretzels from the faux wood bowl on the bar.

Tony recently moved into a manufactured home in a park nearby. "Manufactured home" he thought. "We used to just say 'trailer'". He liked his new home. It was his and his alone.

The walk back took him past the old ginger ale factory which was now a strip mall, home to an upscale pizza place and a coffee shop. Locals still used "ginger ale factory" as a landmark. In New England it is hard to get directions if you don't know the history of a place. Either way everything was closed. Things close early around here.

Tony walked the next half mile to the park and took a left past the office and the mail boxes. All the streets in Tony's park were named after avenues in Manhattan. Tony lived on "Madison". It was kind of ironic that he lived on Madison. Madison was the name of the woman that now owned his house and most of his bank account. Life can be funny sometimes. Not hilarious, but funny. When Tony arrived at his door, he noticed the lights were on at his neighbor's place. He didn't know her very well. She seemed grumpy and she had one of those ankle nipper dogs old ladies seem to like. Tony fumbled with his keys. He really needed to get a locksmith out to fix the door latch. Apparently, his cussing was a little more out loud than he thought it was and his neighbor was soon at her window.

"Are you okay out there?" Her voice sounded like gravel streaming down a wash board.

"I'm fine, just fighting this darn door". He actually did say "darn". "What are you doing up so late?"

"I'm always up this late, I don't sleep"

"I will try to be quieter next time"

About this time the little nipper dog started yapping. You couldn't call it barking, it was yapping.

"Shut up Sparky", she yelled.

"Your dog is called Sparky?"

"Yes, what's it to you?"

"Just asking. You had him long?"

"Her, she's a her! and I've had her since she was a pup. A dog is a much better companion than a person"

Tony decided not to pursue this and find out why a dog was a better companion than a person. He was tired.

"Good night" he said.

"Try not to be so noisy next time".

"Yup"

The sun woke Tony up a little later than he had planned. Not that he had anywhere to go. He already submitted his three job resumes this week that would keep the unemployment people off his back. Nobody is really interested in hiring a salesman this far past his "best by" date anyway. He wasn't worried yet. The trailer was paid for and if he was frugal, he had enough to go a few months between the unemployment checks and the money he had in the bank from selling his motorcycles. Madison let him have his motorcycles, but she kept his dad's watch out of spite. He pretty much had the whole day free.

It was still before noon and already in the nineties with humidity. It was the kind of day where the air is so thick and heavy it feels more like swimming than walking. The trailer was not air conditioned. The only thing to do was sit outside under the awning and sweat.

Tony grabbed a Bud light out the fridge. Hair of the dog. He put a CD of Lightning Hopkins in the boom box and plunked himself in his lawn chair under the awning. The first few phrases of "Bad Luck and Trouble" were coming from the speakers when the same neighbor from last night banged on her window and yelled.

"Turn that down this aint a girly bar"

"That's not girly bar music, That's Lightning Hopkins one of the greatest Texas bluesman ever"

"I don't care- put on Willie Nelson"

"Pshaw", he had no words.

Tony actually did not know the neighbor's name. He only ever spoke to her through the window. He offered her a Bud light and invited her over. She came over with her nippy little yappy dog and sat down next to him.

"My husband worked thirty years at the turnpike taking tolls"

"Did he retire?"

"No, the jerk died eleven years ago. Heart attack."

"Sorry to hear that"

"Not as sorry as I was. That jerk."

Her name was Lorraine and she'd been in that park for ten years. Her husband had enough insurance to buy her this trailer and she had social security and a small pension to live off of. In spite of the gritty demeanor and cigarette voice she was a pretty nice person. Didn't care much for country blues though. Her dog wasn't even that nippy.

She finished her beer and set the empty on the ground. She stared at Tony like she was looking at a car crash and wanted to look away but couldn't.

"So, what brings you here?"

He then remembered he left his car back at the restaurant.

"Last night my shoes brought me here"

That wasn't what she asked. He wasn't ready to talk about it.

Chapter 2

1980 - Graduation Day

Graduation day, finally graduation day. Tony stood in front of his powder blue 1971 Camaro holding his brand-new MBA and smiling like he had a secret only he knew. His parents and Madison were stood across from him to take his picture. Any passing stranger could see the pride in Tony's father's face. Tony was the first generation of his family to graduate from college. His parents both immigrated to the US from Italy before Tony was born. He had his new diploma and new job waiting for him. He was going into sales and marketing at Wang Labs, Wang was hot, business was good. The future looked pretty bright. His new job started in two weeks but for now it was party time. His parents reserved the function room at the Prince Grotto and invited fifty of their best friends to celebrate.

"What's next?" asked his uncle Bob.

"I have three months of training then I will be assigned a territory. I am told this stuff sells itself and I should be able to make 30 or 40K in my first year"

"Let me buy you a drink to celebrate Tony", Uncle Bob liked to buy drinks for people.

"No thanks, I am not much of a drinker".

"Come on kid, celebrate" Uncle Bob was persistent.

"Well, okay one" Tony gave in.

The party went to about eleven that night and Tony found himself alone with Madison.

"When are you going to tell your parents?" asked Madison.

"I thought I'd do it this weekend before we left for the whites. You know how they are, they'll make a big deal out of it"

"It is a big deal, we are getting married", Madison sounded a little exasperated.

"Yeah, but you know how they are, old world." Tony sounded exasperated too.

That weekend Tony and Madison were going to the Mount Washington hotel. The Mount Washington was one of the last of the grand old mountain resorts. Built for a time when people came by train and stayed all summer. Toward the end of world war two the Bretton Woods conference was held there. The hotel was a little worn down but still elegant. Tony hesitated to tell his parents about getting married because they were old world and wanted him to marry an Italian woman, preferably from the old village. Madison was the opposite of that. She could not be more opposite of that. They were going to elope that weekend. The parents would prefer a big, traditional wedding, Tony and Madison did not care for that.

Tony told his father first.

"You can't do that, you'll kill your mother" Tony's father said.

"Can and will, sorry but it's basically done", Tony replied.

Then his father said something in Italian that Tony did not quite pick up. His Italian was not very good. His parents made a point of speaking only English around him growing up. They were proud of their heritage, but they wanted their kid to blend in. What little Italian he had was rapidly fading.

The first round was done. Next, he had to face his mother. He would rather face a charging bear. His mother was four foot eleven in every direction, opinionated, and not afraid to speak her mind. Even his father, rough and tough tannery man that he was, was afraid of her. She was in the kitchen making cannoli shells. The dough was laid out on the marble slab she used for rolling dough for pasta. There was a piece of a broom stick in her hand that she used as a mold to shape the cannoli shells. She had on the same messy white and red apron she always wore. It was stained with years of pasta sauce and olive oil. Tony did not remember a time when she had a different apron. Her white and black hair was tied behind her head in a long pony tail. She stood looking at him and holding the piece of broom stick. Her four foot eleven look every bit of six foot nine from Tony's perspective.

"Ma, I have to talk to you"

"What do you want Antonio"

"Sit down Ma"

"Why, is somebody dying? Is it Aunt Therese?". Italian mothers always expect the worse when it comes to news.

"No one's dying Ma, I am getting married this weekend"

"To who?"

"To Madison Ma, who did you think?"

Tony's mother stood up, all four foot eleven looking all six foot nine. He thought he could see steam coming out of her ears. Not figuratively, literally. She slowly hit her left hand with the broom stick in her right hand. The dough was laid out on the marble dough slab and the oil was still boiling on the stove. Tony was calculating how quickly he could get to the door behind him and also wondering if his affairs were in order. Instead of getting married this weekend Madison will probably be buying a black dress. His mother mumbled something in Italian and turned back to the stove. She wrapped the dough around the end of the broom stick and plunged it into the hot oil.

"Antonio, why are you doing this?"

"She makes me happy Ma"

"She's not one of us"

"You need to get to know her Ma"

"She's not one of us, she will disappoint you"

For now, the discussion was over. At least he wasn't dead, and he figured he had at least thirty years to get his mother back on his side. She was only fifty-five and he was pretty sure she had a long way to go to mellow enough that either the devil or Jesus would want her.

CHAPTER3

THE COFFEE SHOP

Tony finished his beer and went inside. He wanted to shower off the morning's sweat and last night's grime before he walked back to get his car. After a shower and shave he put on some clean jeans and his other Lowell Spinners tee shirt. The walk back took him past the pizza place and the coffee shop. He stopped to watch the lunch crowd as they wandered in and out. No one noticed him, they were all busy with their own thing. Some were plotting how they were going to change the world while others were just trying to figure out whether they would go hiking or boating this week end. Tony reached into his pocket and pulled out the wad of bills that was in there. Years ago, he stopped keeping his bills in his wallet and by now he doesn't remember why. He had two twenties, a ten and a five. The twenties were on the inside of the fold and the ten was in the middle. The five was on the outside. In his younger days he spent a time as a valet parking cars downtown at one of those trendy eateries where the food has funny names, and no one will admit they paid a lot of money to eat food their parents might have scavenged for themselves because it was all they could afford. His boss taught him to fold the money that way so that it didn't look like he had a lot of it. That is not a problem now, he thought with a little chuckle.

"I could use a cup of coffee" He said out loud to no one.

The woman behind the counter looked to be about half of Tony's age. She was dressed in jeans and the coffee shop's logo tee. Her hair was tied back, and she wore glasses with pink rims. There was no line and she recognized Tony but did not know his name.

"Regular coffee? Large?"

"Yes, thanks"

"I haven't seen you in here for a few days"

"I've been busy". Truth was, he'd been hiding in his trailer. "What do I owe you?"

"On the house, you look like you could use it"

"Thanks, do I look that bad?"

"Your eyes look like brake lights, and not in a good way"

Coffee tastes even better when it's free. Tony's spirits were lifted a little. Everyone in the coffee shop was reading their laptops and iPads. Tony had enough of that, he was happy to find an actual paper newspaper, the Boston Globe, someone had let on a table. He liked everything about a real newspaper. He liked the feel of the paper in his hands, the crinkle sound it made when you turned a page, even the ink stains on his fingers. The Globe was broadsheet format, big and unwieldy. The other newspaper in town was tabloid format, easier to handle, especially when seated in public. Tony preferred the broadsheet. To him it felt more substantial like the news in it would be more important. His Catholic upbringing taught him that everything good needs to be suffered for.

The news this day was more of the same. Somebody did something bad to some one else. Some politician was going to protect everyone from whatever was perceived as evil today. Tony turned to the sports page. It was baseball season and the Red Sox were in third place, four games out. There was a sanity in baseball that wasn't found in the rest of life. There were rules that everyone agreed to. There was a score, standings and statistics. An E.R.A. was an E.R.A. Things were black and white. No one could lie about the outcome of a game or twist the statistics to prove their thesis. It was what it was. Tony liked that.

He imagined some day he would sit down with his grand children and explain to them what a newspaper was and that at one time it was really made out of paper. He hadn't seen his grand children since they were very little. He hoped to be able to see them soon. He would take them outside and play catch when they were big enough.

The coffee was gone, and the sports page fully read. It was time to get the car.

"Thanks for coffee, tell Sandy I said 'hi'". Sandy owned the coffeeshop.

"Come back Saturday night, we have music"

"Maybe I will do that"

"You know, I don't actually know your name"

"Tony, yours?"

"Jessica"

"Maybe I will see you Saturday Jessica"

The car was still where he left it behind The Embers. Not that that was a surprise. No one was going to steal a twenty odd year-old Buick Riviera and it wasn't parked anywhere that meant it was going to be towed. He bought this car for five hundred bucks. It was a good five hundred buck car. One tire was pretty bald, so he went to the junk yard and got one that was good enough. That's all he had to do to make it drivable. All told he had five hundred and twenty bucks into the car. It was a good five hundred and twenty buck car. It wasn't the Audi he used to drive but Tony was just as happy to have this car.

The gas gauge was somewhere between 'fumes' and 'get out and walk' so he decided to go next door to Sid's little independent gas station. Sid, the owner, was pumping gas. It was the cheapest place in town and also the only place that wasn't self serve. The gas was a no name brand, but Sid assured everyone it came from the same tanks in Chelsea that the guy across the street used. Tony didn't care, he wanted the cheapest. It could be swamp water for all he cared, as long as his car ran.

"Sid, can I get ten bucks worth and check the oil?"

"Ten bucks? Ten bucks won't get you far"

"I ain't going far". That was true. His plan was to drive the two miles back to the park.

Sid opened the hood to check the oil. He pulled out the dipstick and wiped it with the old rag he had hanging from his belt.

"The oil looks good. when did you change it last?"

"Whenever the guy I bought the car from did" was Tony's reply.

"You should change it" Sid admonished. "This car is practically a classic, take care of it"

"Classic piece of junk" was Tony's only response.

Ten buck's worth of gas would last Tony most of the week. Half the time he walked everywhere. There is not a lot of commuting when you don't have a job. Tony paid Sid and headed home.

Lorraine was watering her three cherry tomato plants when Tony pulled his car up to the trailer. The yappy dog must have been inside, Tony didn't see it anywhere.

When Tony got out of his car Lorraine looked up and said "Some guy came by looking for you. Well dressed, if you care"

"Oh yeah? did he leave a message?"

"He left this card", Lorraine held a business card out to him with a shaky hand.

Tony looked at the card, spit on the ground and put the card in his pocket.

CHAPTER 4

TONY'S FIRST DAY AT WORK 1980

Tony's first day at his new job was chaos. No one seemed to know what he was to do. Mike, the manager who hired him, was on a trip to visit a big customer and left no instructions. After meeting with the human resources people and filling out the usual forms he was shown to his cubical and left on his own. His cubical was one of those modular office system deals that were popular at that time. There was a desk hanging off of the divider, a shelf for books, a small two drawer file cabinet and a chair with some unidentifiable stains. The desk had a terminal attached to a Wang VS system and a manual. The last occupant of this cube was probably a smoker. The key legends were barely legible with tobacco ash that he hoped he would be able to clean up.

The company had a paging system that never seemed to shut up. After a while Tony noticed the same names went by all the time. They must be pretty important he thought.

Tony looked up to see someone standing in the opening to his cube.

"Hey, you're the new guy" the stranger said.

"Tony, what's your name?"

"Bob, I'm the department tech guy"

"Nice meeting you Bob"

"I am here to set up your phone"

"Go for it"

Bob climbed under the desk and was messing with the wires and plugs for a few minutes. Tony looked over there and thought to himself "Maybe Bob should have been a plumber". That made him chuckle a little.

"I have to go to the wiring closet and move some wires around, I will be right back. You see,....... "

Tony interrupted what looked like was going to be a dissertation "Okay, thanks". Tony wasn't sure that he cared, he just wanted his phone to work.

True to his word Bob came back in a few minutes.

"Try the phone, it should be working".

Tony picked up the phone and listened for the dial tone. "Yup, it is. Thanks."

"I've been here ten years." Bob was starting a conversation.

"That's nice". Tony wasn't interested but he nothing else to do. Bob seemed like a nice enough guy except for the smell. Tony was dressed in a sports coat, slacks and his red power tie. Bob had jeans, white sneakers and a Grateful Dead tee shirt under which his ample belly would sometimes peek. Tony was "on his way up" and Bob was plateaued at best. At least that's the way Tony saw it. He had big plans for himself. He wanted his first million before he was thirty and to be at least a director if not a vice president at this company, or a better one. Tony was ambitious.

"Do you like D&D?" Bob asked.

"I don't know what that is" Tony was hoping it wasn't something weird

"Dungeons and Dragons, it's a role-playing card game"

Oh crap, it was something weird. "I've never played"

"You should come over and play sometime"

"Yeah, sure" and silently "When hell freezes over", Tony was not enthusiastic.

"Some of the guys are going to the Knickerbocker club for lunch, you want joint us?"

Tony didn't know what a Knickerbocker club was. "What they heck", he thought.

"Sure"

"I will grab you when we are leaving"

"Thanks", Tony turned back to his work.

The Knickerbocker Club was a social club in a nearby neighborhood. At lunch time they let anyone who could pay in. It was dark in there and it smelled like stale cigarettes and beer. The walls were paneled with fake mahogany and sports memorabilia. There was a signed photo of Carl Yazstremski that Tony was lusting over. Yaz was Tony's favorite member of the '67 Sox. Tony played left field in little league. The floor was red and white tiles. The white tiles were more like yellow tiles now. Most of the furniture was aging and worn out as were most of the daytime staff. There was a big room off to one side with picnic tables where everyone ate. The end of the room had a bar and next to the bar was a window through which you could order food. The club sold a variety of sandwiches and deep-fried things providing job security for the local cardiologists. Most of Tony's coworkers ordered steak and cheese and a couple of beers. Tony had a grilled cheese and a Coke.

Some guys shot darts and some played pool. Most sat, ate and talked. The talk usually revolved around sports, TV, or complaining about the job.

Tony looked around at the people he came with. His coworkers were a very eclectic group. They ranged in age from low twenties to mid sixties. There were more men than women but the person who wielded the most power in the department was Mike's secretary Alice. He relied on her for a lot and she acted as his consigliere. Bob said that the last guy to get on her bad side was moved to the "Siberian office". Tony didn't know what that meant but he had an idea that he did not want to go there. Some of them had been at the company for a long time. Some were fairly new there. Bob introduced Tony around to everyone.

Tony's immediate supervisor was a thirty something man who smoked a lot. Everyone called him "Guido" though his real name was John. He had been with the company only about two years and had just been made section manager. Section managers had a "real office" with a door and a window. John reported to Mike and Tony was hired to work for him. Tony now occupied Guido's old cube.

"How are you enjoying your first day?" Guido asked

"I am settling in" Tony was not sure how else to answer that. So far, he read a manual and found where to get coffee. He really hadn't done any work.

"Do you like old cars?" Guido asked Tony.

"I do, I always wanted a '63 coupe. Maybe someday I will be able to get one"

"Maybe you will, I have a '59 T-Bird- I'll give you a ride next time I bring it in."

"That's a nice car" Tony was impressed.

"We are doing a sales pitch to Middlesex bank tomorrow, why don't you tag along. You don't know the product yet so just observe. Ask Alice for a copy of the presentation. You can study it" Guido switched to business mode.

"Will do, thanks"

That gave Tony something to do for the afternoon. He asked Alice for a copy of the presentation. She smiled and went into teh little room behind her desk. Tony could hear the sounds of the copy machine. After a bit she came out with stack of paper neatly arranged and stapled. She was very nice to him and not as scary as he had been led to believe. Then again, lion fish are pretty until they sting you. Tony took the papers back to his little cube and studied them. The afternoon went by quicker than the morning. Tony studied the presentation then studied the manuals for the products they were pitching. He wanted to be ready for tomorrow. Bets of all, Bob left him alone.

CHAPTER 5

THE CARD

Tony sat at the kitchen table staring at the card that Lorraine had given him for two and a half Bud Lights. The condensation from the cans made a little puddle on the Formica tabletop. That might have been the only clean spot on the table. Maybe he should call, but why? The last time they spoke was not the most pleasant time and probably not a high point in either man's life. Depending on how you define "high point".

The microwave beeped to tell him that his Hot Pocket was ready. Tony put the card back in his pocket and clicked the TV on. He didn't have cable, but his antenna pulled in a couple of local channels.

He didn't need cable if he wanted to watch ESPN or the Sox he could go down to The Embers. Danny the bartender would let him sit all night if he was quiet and bought a couple of beers.

The news was on. Tony liked watching the news. Watching the news made him feel better about having fewer days ahead than behind.

"This world is circling the drain" he thought.

He felt sorry for his grandkids and if he ever saw them, he would apologize for leaving them such a screwed-up world. His favorite part of the news was the weather forecasters. The weather people were always so perky. The worse the weather the happier they seemed to be. One of the weather people on this channel taught meteorology at the university nearby. One time he saw her at in the bar with her husband and some friends. He did not dare to go over and introduce himself. He was not so far in his cups that he didn't know he was too far to be talking to someone like that. It's too bad, he really wanted to tell her how much he liked the way she presented the weather. In his salesman's life he learned to appreciate good presentation skills. This night the weather person was excited about tropical storm "Walter" that was just forming in the Atlantic. All the models said it might head up the east coast of the U.S. They always made a big deal about these things and Tony wondered if people were getting complacent because of all the wolf crying. Someday a really bad one will hit, and no one will be ready. Not totally ready for sure. There is always a big run on milk, bread and batteries before a storm so that will be covered. Anyway, it was days before he had to worry about it.

The national news was next. It seemed to Tony like the world was on a loop that just repeated itself over and over. Whoever was in charge got lazy and just kept cutting and pasting the same thing over and over again with the occasional name change. There's another thing he'd have to apologize to his grandkids for. Tony shut the T.V. off.

"Come outside a look at this" Lorraine was yelling just outside of his door.

Tony got up from his la-z-boy and walked over to the screen door.

"Look at what?"

Lorraine was standing by the picnic table and pointing. Standing is a term used loosely. It was more of a swaying and leaning.

"It's them damn chemtrails. The government is putting chemicals in the air to control our minds"

Tony looked up in the sky. The setting sun had made the contrail of passing jet glow like neon in the sky.

"That's just a jet contrail" Tony said

"No no no, it's chemtrails"

Lorraine was not going to be convinced and Tony knew that when she was this far into her nightly "comforts", as she called them, there was no arguing.

"It's not just a jet. I read this on the inter webs at the library. The government puts chemicals in the air to mind control us. You can look it up. One fellow in Texas said that he was straight as the horizon and this chemical made him gay."

"You want I should make you a tin foil hat?" Tony asked.

"Don't mess with me Tony, you're starting to look a little off yourself"

"I'm fine. Maybe you should go inside and sleep"

"I aint sleeping, that's when the get you"

"Okay then, at least sit down at the table, do you want anything to eat? I have some nacho chips"

"Can I have a beer? I saw you walk in earlier with some Bud Light"

"I'll get you a beer"

Tony didn't have so much spare money that he wanted to give away such a valuable commodity, but it was Lorraine. He grabbed two beers from his fridge and brought out the bag of nacho chips and put them on the picnic table.

"Did you call that guy?" Lorraine asked.

"No, I didn't"

"He looked important like he was from the CIA or something. He was shady I could tell. Wouldn't look me in the eye. You're not some kind of spy, are you?"

"Yeah, I'm a double naught spy. I just live in this trailer as a cover." Tony hoped the sarcasm came through but in Lorraine's state, who knew?

"Don't be a jerk."

"Sorry" He guessed the sarcasm did come through.

"He's not a spy just a guy I used to work with. I haven't spoken to him in a long time"

"You going to call him?"

"I don't think so."

"Call him, maybe he owes you money"

"He doesn't owe me money". That was true. Tony owed him something though.

"He looked rich. He dressed really sharp and drove up in a Porsche. "

Tony tipped his beer up to drain the last little bit out and crushed the can in his hand. Got to love aluminum cans. He tossed the can over toward the barrel and stood up. He stared for a second at Lorraine. He couldn't be mad at her. He just did not want to talk to this guy.

"Lorraine- do you know the difference between a Porsche and a porcupine? "

"No, I don't"

"Good night Lorraine" Tony went inside.

CHAPTER 6

TONY'S FIRST SALE CALL

Guido came by Tony's cube just after Tony started his second cup of coffee.

"Ready?" Guido asked.

"Yup"

"Let's go. Remember you are there to observe. You don't need to say anything."

"Got it. I reviewed the presentation and the docs last night" Tony tried to show he had initiative.

"That's great, just keep quiet, especially when I am closing"

"Yup"

The customer was about a one-hour drive away. They took Guido's Mercedes. Guido smoked like a volcano, so the inside of his windshield had that yellow film smoker's cars always have, the whole thing smelled like an ashtray. Tony didn't smoke much and the smell and the smoke from Guido's cigarette made him a little nauseated by the time they got to the customer.

"Are you okay?" Guido asked.

"A little wobbly but I will be fine."

This customer was a bank that wanted to automate their office. 'Office automation' was the hot term at the time. They wanted to make their reports and paper work easier to manage. The upper managers hoped that they could even cut back on office staff. Tony and Guido were met in the lobby by a tall sixty plus year old balding man in a blue suit, black wing tips and red tie. He escorted them upstairs to the executive area and introduced them around. Everyone in the room was a vice president. It was a bank, at a bank everyone who isn't a worker is a vice president. Guido stood by the overhead projector and got out the slide deck for the presentation. Everyone in the room listened politely to Guido's practiced sales pitch. Bankers always listen politely. It was a different world from the high-tech world Tony was used to. In his world everyone was in a hurry and would often cut a presenter short to get to the point. Bankers seems to have all day to listen. Almost no one fell asleep.

The tall balding man that met them in the lobby stood up and said "Thank you for that presentation, it was very impressive"

A shorter, fatter man with a curled-up mustache next to him, who up to now hadn't said a word, joined in and asked, "When can we get a bid proposal?"

"I can have one for you early next week. We could install the system in a month an have you up and running in two" Guido was shifting into closing mode.

The grey-haired man with glasses at the head of the table said "We look forward to it"

Tony looked around the room. "Any more questions?"

The only woman in the room raised a hand. She looked to be in her early thirties and was dressed very conservatively. Not much differently dressed than the surrounding gaggle of middle aged and old men.

"What happens if the power goes out in the middle of the day? I have a big typing pool under me and don't want to lose a lot of work to a power failure. When we are typing directly on paper it never goes away when the power fails" She asked.

Guido was ready for this. "We have a saying. Save early and save often. Whatever you saved last will still be in the system"

"That sounds like a pain in the neck. I have to stop often and save stuff? How long does that take?"

"Not long"

"I don't like it" She wasn't convinced.

"We have a feature coming out that will automatically save at fixed intervals". Tony remembered seeing that in the manual. Guido gave Tony the "I told you to be quiet" look.

"That feature comes out next fall" Guido said.

"Maybe we should wait for then to do this" the woman replied.

The gaggle of men started talking among themselves and gesturing spasmodically. Then the gray-haired man, who apparently was the alpha banker, said. "That's a good idea, maybe we should revisit this in a few months. Thanks for coming by. We will spend some time discussing this and get back to you soon."

The tall balding man escorted Guido and Tony back to the lobby.

"We'll get back to you"

"Thanks"

Tony and Guido went back to the Mercedes. When they got to the car Guido lit up a cigarette. His face was red, and he was mumbling beneath his breath. Tony started reviewing his Boy Scout first aid training and trying to remember what to do if someone was having a heart attack or was speaking in tongues to himself. He was pretty sure they covered the latter in Sunday school.

"I told you not to say anything!"

"Sorry, I thought…."

"You thought, you thought- did I tell you to think? I told you to watch and listen. I was the close to closing that deal now they want to wait until the next release!"

"But that is only a few months out"

"One thing you'll learn is nothing, absolutely nothing, gets done on time. This deal was going to make my quota. Now it's delayed if not blown entirely. They're probably on the phone with IBM right now"

Tony shut up. It was a long quiet ride back to the office. Guido didn't even turn on talk radio. So much for Tony's meteoric rise. It looks like his career is derailed before it even started.

"How did the sales call go?" Bob wasn't good at reading faces.

"It could have been better" Tony growled a short answer, not offering any more than that.

"How so?" Bob wasn't good at hearing nuance either.

"I could have kept my mouth shut and not blown it." Tony did not really want to discuss it, especially with Bob.

Tony kept to himself the rest of the day and read some more manuals. Just as he was shutting off his light and getting ready to leave Guido came by.

"Here it comes" Tony thought to himself "Pack your stuff and go home"

"You got a minute?" Guido asked.

"Sure"

"Walk with me"

"Ok"

Tony followed Guido to the elevator and they took the elevator to the first floor. They left the elevator and started walking toward the older building. The complex they were in consisted of a new eleven story tower and an older two-story building attached it. The older building contained the human resources offices among other things. Tony was pretty sure he was being walked out. You don't get to screw up a lot in this business and a new guy is on probation for the first ninety days. Tony was surprised when they turned into the executive dining room. The suits had their own dining room and did not eat cafeteria style food at formica tables in the employee lunch room with the unwashed masses. Their dining room had tables with table clothes, real silverware, candles at every table and a wait staff. Guido gestured to one of the tables and they sat down. A waiter came over and asked if he could get any drinks. It was after five and all they served were drinks.

Guido said "Bring us two Jim Beams, rocks"

Tony protested" I am not much of a drinker"

Guido looked at the waiter and held up two fingers.

"Look kid, I over reacted today. This quarter is not going as well as we had forecast, and we are all under pressure to pull in the numbers. I think you have the potential to be a good salesman. You're personable, you're learning the product line and you are well spoken. "

The waiter showed up with the drinks and set them on the table. Guido picked his up and held it up to Tony. Tony raised his and they clanked glasses together.

"Here's to a better day tomorrow, kid. I can read people. That woman at the bank trusts you. I could tell by the way she looked at you. I want you to try to make an appointment with her. Invite her here to look at the prototypes of the next release. Maybe we can salvage this."

Guido made a circular gesture with his hands indication to waiter he wanted another round. Tony stared to protest but between the warmth of the whiskey and the relief of not getting fired his internal protest motor was silenced.

The next two hours were a blur in Tony's memory. They talked sports, selling, politics, selling and of course, selling. All over a few more rounds. Somehow Tony made it back to the apartment. Madison opened the door. A wobbly Tony poured in.

"Long day at work?"

"I thought I was going to get fired." Tony told the whole story about the bank, the bald guy, the alpha banker and almost giving Guido a heart attack.

"So, is this an 'I'm glad I wasn't fired' drunk or something else?"

"My boss pulled me into the exec dining room to talk things out. He likes his whiskey and will not drink alone."

"Get cleaned up an I'll make up the couch. You're sleeping out here tonight. You smell like a saloon and you snore like a freight train when you drink"

"Fair enough"

Tony curled up on the couch and thought about the day and what he may do tomorrow.

CHAPTER 7

TONY TAKES LORRAINE TO AN APPOINTMENT.

Tony was awakened by the noise of a truck's back up beeper right outside his window. He looked at his clock. It was 9:30. It was still dark in his bedroom because he had nailed old blankets up in front of the windows. If he didn't have a job to go to, he didn't see the need of letting old Mr. Sol wake him up any earlier than necessary. His first thought was to run out the front door and see what was going on, but he was not wearing any pants or a shirt. His neighbors did not ever do him any harm to the extent that they needed to see a thing like that. He put on his sweat pants and picked up the tee shirt that was laying on the floor by his bed. After he rubbed the sleep out his eyes and put on a baseball cap to hide his bed head he went to the door. Outside was a flat bed truck picking up Lorraine's car.

"What's going on?" Tony asked.

Lorraine was standing outside her place in a robe. Her hair was tied up in a cap and she was wearing bunny slippers. She did not look like a bunny slipper person.

"The state says I shouldn't drive anymore. Fricken car doesn't run anyways so they are hauling it away, I got a hundred bucks for it"

"How will you get around?"

"I'll manage. I can walk"

"Call me if you need a ride" Tony didn't mean it but its what people say.

"How about today? I need a ride to the doctor. This leg..."

"Uh, sure- what time?"

"2:00 and don't be late. I don't like to be late. Do you have one of those GPS things? leave it home, they can track you with those"

"No GPS. I'll wear my tin foil hat"

Well, Tony had something to do this afternoon.

The passenger side door creaked when Tony opened it for Lorraine. Tony did not remember the last time he actually used that door. No one ever rides with him. Lorraine got in and sat down.

"Fasten your seat belt Lorraine"

"I hate them damn things. You could crash into the water and they would keep you from getting out. I never use them. They're a government conspiracy"

"There's a law. You have to. I can't afford a ticket"

"I hate them"

Lorraine fastened her seat belt like she was punching someone who was lying on the ground. Tony was both surprised at her strength and surprised the latch didn't break.

"Where's your doctor?" he asked.

"Over on Fletcher Street, next to the spot where the bakery used to be"

Oddly enough Tony knew what bakery she meant. "I've lived here too long" he said, but not very loudly. Lorraine didn't hear him. She was fiddling with the radio looking for her talk radio show. She got all of her news from the talk radio show.

"Long time listener, first time caller" She found it.

"When is the city going to do something about all them homeless guys in the park? "The caller and the host both went on about the no-good homeless guys and how the city should do something. Nether made any sense.

"This guy really knows his stuff" Lorraine was impressed. Tony didn't want to argue so he tried to change the subject.

"You mind if I ask what's wrong with your leg?"

"Yes, I do mind. None of your business"

"Ok, your call.

"Bad knees, too much skiing when I was younger"

"You skied?"

"I was great. Could have made the Olympics but I got married and my husband didn't want me to try. He thought it was stupid. Then thirty years later the puke up and dies and I have bad knees. That's probably more than you wanted to know"

The doctor's office was in a row of town house offices. Tony sat himself outside on a bench by Lorraine's doctor's office to wait for her. The weather was pretty nice, there were few clouds and the temperature was comfortable. It was a nice day to be outside. He sat staring at the bank across the street. It was a branch of the bank that was one of his very first customers as a sales guy. "Huh" he thought, "At least they are still in business". At the other end of the parking lot was a package store. A packie the locals called it. Tony gave some thought to maybe wondering over and buying a single for the wait. It was a bit of a walk, so he lit a cigarette instead. Tony let himself have one cigarette a day and this was it.

"Hey buddy, read the sign- you can't smoke within twenty-five feet of the door"

Tony was looking at a twenty something year old hipster. Complete with ironic mustache and pork pie hat. His first instinct was to get up off that bench and punch him in the face. He went with his second instinct.

"Bite me" Tony was nothing if not eloquent.

The hipster looked at Tony with what only be described as cross between contempt and indignation.

"Put it out"

"Bite me"

Just then Lorraine came out of the doctor's office.

"Tony, you gotta take me to get pills. "

Tony flicked his cigarette in the direction of the hipster and helped Lorraine get in the car.

"Pick that up"

"Bite me"

As they drove off Lorraine asked" What was that about"

"Just a disagreement about smoking. What pharmacy do you need"?

"The one by Friendly's"

"Lived here too long" Tony said to no one and not out loud.

Chapter 8

Tony Has A Meeting

Tony was at work earlier than normal in spite of the fog and haze over his brain from his impromptu after-hours performance review with Guido. "Guido can put away the whiskey" Tony thought on his way up the stairs. He wanted to review the specs again and get ready to meet with the bank woman. Once eight o'clock came that damn paging system started up again. It always seemed to be the same names. It had become a background noise and Tony did not notice the first time his name came by.

"Tony Sincero call 5029"

"Tony Sincero call 5029"

"What the heck?" he thought.

Tony dialed the number. It was Guido. He was in Mike's office.

"Tony- come up to Mike's office."

"On my way". Tony had not seen Mike since his interview. He seemed nice enough then. He wasn't sure what he would be like now that he was on the job.

Tony walked into Mike's office. Mike was behind a mahogany desk. Most folks had either modular cubes or steel and formica desks. Guido was sitting in a chair to the right of Mike. Tony noticed a number of "things in lucite" on the credenza in Mike's office. It was traditional after a successful product release to pass out some token of the product embedded in lucite. Mike had trophies going back almost to the beginning. He started out as a technician in the machine shop and kept getting promoted over the years. Loyalty was encouraged at this company. Mike had black rimmed glasses and dark hair. He wore a blue suit, but his tie was loose, and the jacket was a little wrinkled. Tony didn't notice back in the interview, but he did not look to be that much older than he, not as old as he would expect anyway.

"Hi Tony, have a seat"

"Morning Mike, morning Guido"

"Guido and I were just discussing the customer meeting yesterday." Mike said.

"Again. I apologize for speaking out of turn" Tony replied.

"Don't worry about it. I think we can use that to our advantage" Mike interrupted Tony.

"How so?"

"I had Alice invite the woman you met to come for a demo of our future products. She will be here at one o'clock. We want you to meet with her. If you can convince her, we think she can in turn convince her bosses"

"I will try my best"

"You will DO your best". There was just the smallest hint of threat in Mike's voice.

Tony left the meeting more scared than when he went in. He would almost rather they fired him. Bob was waiting outside the office talking to Alice.

"You need me to set up a demo of 3.0?" It wasn't a question, really. Mike had already told Alice to get Bob to set it up. "That's going to be a lot of work. I may miss lunch". Tony was pretty sure Bob didn't miss too many lunches, or dinners, or beers.

"I appreciate the help. It's important" Tony said.

"I will set it up in the big conference room by the front it's the only place with the connections. Porter has his weekly meeting there you will need to clear him out"

"Porter?"

"Yup, Porter. Good luck" Bob smirked a little when he said this.

Porter was the other section manager. He and Guido were rivals. The talk around the office was that Porter expected to be in charge of everyone and was put out when Guido was made section manager. Tony didn't listen to office gossip usually, but Bob's tone and smirk made him nervous.

"Move my meeting? Why?" Porter didn't even look up from his papers.

"Guido and I have a customer demo to do in that room"

"Not my problem. Who are you anyway?"

"I'm Tony. I'm new here. I work for Guido."

"Tell me when I should start caring" Still not looking up.

"Look, I'm sorry to inconvenience you but I need to do this" Tony was adamant.

"Not my problem, find another room" Porter was stubborn.

"Bob tells me that is the only room with the right connections". Tony was starting to understand why Bob chuckled a little when he said, "Good luck".

"Well then I guess you are just out of luck"

Tony didn't know what to do. It was clear he didn't have the juice to win this argument. It was also clear that his job might depend on this. He hated office politics. He knew this wasn't about him. It was about Porter and Guido. Maybe he should not have mentioned his name.

He went back and found Bob. "Are you sure we can't use a different room?"

"I am, at least not on this floor"

"So what other floor?"

"The exec meeting room by the dining room would work"

"How do I get that?"

"Ask Alice".

Alice and Porter went way back. They had history. Tony wasn't sure what kind of hornet's nest he might be about to stir up by asking for her help. He explained to her that Porter was a little reluctant to give up the conference room. He did not include the tone of their conversation.

"Can you get me the exec meeting room?"

"No, but I can get you Porter's room"

"How?"

"Go back to your desk"

Tony went back to his desk. Pretty soon he heard Porter being paged to call 5029. Shortly after that his phone rang.

"You're all set. Bob is setting up the equipment now". It was Alice.

"Thanks, how did you do that?"

"I'm Alice".

Right about then Porter walked by Tony's cube. He gave Tony the finger. "Great" Tony thought "I've made Porter an enemy".

The bank woman showed up exactly at one o'clock. Bank people were very reliable. Her name was Sandy. She wore a blue suit, wire rimmed glasses and tied her hair back in a bun. It was like she was trying to look as much like one of the banker guys as she could. She carried a brief case and no purse. She was younger than Tony at first thought, maybe twenty-five.

Tony introduced himself again.

"I remember you from yesterday. You were pretty quiet" Sandy said.

"I'm new here. I just graduated this year. MBA from B.U. I wasn't supposed to say much yesterday. I am still in training"

"Sorry about that thing yesterday, I kind of ruined your whole pitch"

"Not a problem. You have legit concerns. Let me show you where we are going. I think we will have all the features you want by the time you are fully up and running"

"I have to be honest. It's not the features. I have a group of twenty typists. Mostly woman, some single mothers. The vice presidents think with your product we can get rid of at least five of them. I don't want to get rid of anybody. They all have families"

Tony saw what he was up against now.

"Look, I can't promise you anything about what the suits may do. I can tell you that it does not usually work out that way." Tony saw an opening.

"Easy for you to say, how do you know?"

"I did some case studies for my MBA program. Once they see how easy it is to generate documents and make changes, they will want to generate more documents. It's human nature. We have noticed that among our customers the work seems to grow to fit the resources. "Tony was not sure he wasn't lying.

"So….."

"Suits like to think they are above this type of work. They are not going to do their own typing, but they love to have their names on stuff"

"That makes sense", Sandy was warming up to the program.

"Let me show you the next version" Tony went on to demonstrate the features of the next version. In the process he found out more about Sandy and developed a connection. She asked a lot of good questions and was quick to pick up on the workings of the product. Tony was sure that she was a lot smarter than the suits he met. By the end of the meeting he was sure that she was happier with the product and trusted Tony.

"I will go back to the office and discuss this with my management, we will get back to you."

"Thanks, have a safe ride back"

Tony left Sandy in the lobby and walked back to his area feeling pretty good. He went and found Bob to let him know he could break down the demo gear. He swung by Porter's office on his way back to his cube to tell him the conference room was open and thank him. Porter gave him the finger but otherwise didn't say anything or even look up. Tony wondered what Alice did to get him the room.

Around five o'clock Tony was packing to go home when Mike walked by his cube and pointed at him.

"Come with me kid"

"Okay"

He followed Mike down to the first floor and over to the exec dinning room. Guido was already in there drinking a whiskey and there were two more whiskies on the table. They sat Tony down.

"I don't know how you did it kid. The bank guys called and wanted us to submit the proposal."

They raised their glasses and Tony raised his.

"A toast to the kid"

Glasses clanked, the whiskey went down like smoky lemonade. Tony took the time to roll it around his mouth and notice the warmth as it slid down his throat. He was beginning to like being in sales.

Tony told them the whole story about the typing pool and not wanting to lay any one off and how he convinced Sandy that bringing in their product may actual result in more work.

"How do you know that Tony? The thing about more work? We are always pitching efficiency and cost reduction" Mike asked.

"Part of that was true and part of it made up. I didn't promise it. There are a couple of case studies we used in one of my MBA classes where they found that rather than reducing work load new tools sometimes increase workload."

"Find those. It is a good factoid to have in just these cases" Guido chimed in.

Mike followed "I want you to get some data and put together a slide deck the guys can use for that situation. I don't want them using it always. We don't want scare the upper management guys, but it is good for lower level people"

Tony said "I will dig that out"

The conversation devolved to sports and politics from there and Tony spent another night on the couch.

CHAPTER 9

TENOR DREAMS

Tony remembered his conversation with woman at the coffee shop. Jessica? He wasn't sure. It was Saturday night and they did not have a cover charge, so he decided he would go over there and hear some music. In his college days when a friend lent him a John Prine record and it awoke an appreciation of folk music, he never realized he had, before that he was more into heavy metal. The parking lot at the coffee shop is small and Tony had to wait for an old guy and his pizza in a Cadillac to pull out of a space. "Nice Caddy" he thought. When he got into the coffee shop the only place left to sit was the couch along the very back. The shop decorated in what Tony liked to call "artsy modern". There were some high tables along the window and lower tables through the middle. Everything looked like it escaped from Ikea. There was a nice baby grand in one corner by the wine bar. They didn't serve beer here but that served wine and a couple of fancy kinds of drinks. Tony preferred the coffee. They had a lot of different coffees and he and become addicted to a couple of them. He also liked the pastries. They were baked on the premises and different every day depending on what fresh ingredients could be gotten that day. The musician that night was set up next to the piano. He played solo sitting on a tall stool through a small P.A. system. It could have been louder, Tony would not have minded. Tony couldn't see the player very well from were he sat because there was a row of high tables at the back of the room between him and the player, but he could hear well enough, except when the Scrabble people got loud. There was a table of people to his left playing Scrabble while they listened. They were generally quiet but once in a while would get loud. "It's all community" Tony thought, he didn't mind. Jessica, that was indeed her name, was working behind the coffee counter. Funny, Tony never really paid much attention to her before. He noticed that she was actually older than he first thought, older than the kids that worked there. She was a lot closer to his age than to their ages. There was even a touch of grey here and there in her hair. Tony went up to the counter when the line had gone away.

"Hey, you came- how are you?" Jessica waited on him.

"None the worse for the wear I suppose"

"What can I get you?"

"Mocha decaf and one of those big chocolate chip cookies please"

The player was playing a particularly quiet song and the sound of the espresso machine drowned it out.

"He's pretty good."

"Yup, he comes here about three times a year. He drives all the way up from Pennsylvania. Here's your coffee"

"Thanks. Pennsylvania? That's a long way to play for tips"

"He has friends up here" Jessica replied.

Tony took his cookie and his coffee back to the couch. Someone left today's Globe, so Tony had some reading material. He started reading the sports page when something the player said caught his attention. He mentioned being in Washington state and meeting a woman who lived in a bus. "Maybe I could live in a bus". He did not realize he said it out loud and that Jessica had come over and sat next to him.

"I'm on break" She said.

"Have a seat"

"I already did"

"I guess you heard me just now"

"I did, you want to live in a bus?"

"Why not? Think of the benefits. If your neighbor is a jerk, you just fire that sucker up and move. You don't even have to pack your stuff. There's plenty of windows. If you put the flashers on everyone around has to stop. The perks are endless"

"Didn't you tell me you lived in a mobile home? What part of mobile don't you understand?"

"It's a manufactured home. Mobile is kind of a misnomer. Plus, a bus has its own motor and stuff. You need a truck to move a mobile home"

"You want to move?"

"Sometimes I do. I realized today I have lived here too long. Do you know I can remember when this was a derelict ginger ale factory and trains actually ran behind there?"

"I remember that, it wasn't all that long ago"

"I bet those kids don't remember that" Tony gestured toward the counter.

"That guy playing remembers when steam trains came through here."

"Really?"

"Look at him, he might". Jessica smiled. Tony noticed she had a nice smile.

"After you get off work do you want to grab a drink?"

"I can't. Baby sitter."

"You have kids?"

"I have grandkids and they live with me. Long story"

"Maybe another time"

"Yup, another time"

"I have grandkids. I have not seen them since they were babies, they live in Ohio"

"Why don't you go there and see them?" Jessica asked.

"Long story too. My daughter isn't talking to me right now."

"Go there and make her talk to you. Life is short"

"Shorter every day." Tony was increasingly aware of this.

"My grandkids live with me because their mother is not well. I would never estrange her though. I just want her to get better"

"My daughter is okay. She just doesn't want to talk to me. It's my own fault, I suppose"

"You don't have to talk about it"

"Thanks, I really don't want to"

It was ten o'clock already. Time flies when you have no where to be. The player was introducing his last song was thanking everyone for listening and thanking the shop for having him. Tony reached in his pocket and took out his folded bills. Somewhere in there was a five, he hoped. The tip jar was all the way over the other side of the room on the piano right next to the player. He hoped to sneak over there and throw in a tip without being noticed. He wasn't sure if he did not want anyone to see him tipping or he didn't want anyone to see him only tip five bucks. Some day he would figure it out for himself.

"Thank you". He was noticed. The musician was sitting down about five feet from him. He looked to be in his sixties, He had a beard and longish hair that was very white. Tony looked at his guitar on his lap and noticed it only had four strings. "Hmmm, not six strings" he thought. "This is different, kind of cool". From were he was sitting in the back he did not notice a difference.

"Thank you for the songs. I liked the one about the bus lady"

"It's a true story. We met her on a trip through Washington. She was pretty interesting. everything in the song really happened." The player replied.

"Cool, are all your songs true stories?"

"Not all, though there is a grain of truth in most of them."

"What kind of guitar is that? I didn't notice until now that it was different"

"It's called a Tenor guitar. Some people call it a lazy man's guitar because it only has four strings"

Tony looked closely at the guitar and thought about it for a while. It didn't look any easier to play to him.

"How is it a lazy man's guitar because it only has four strings? You only have four fingers to push them down with anyway. Violins only have four strings are they a lazy man's instrument?" Tony asked.

"So, they say"

"How long have you been writing songs?"

"Pretty much all my life. I wrote my first song at six. It was parody of the Mickey Mouse club theme and involved broccoli. Not my best work. I've written hundreds though only a few them make it to the show"

"You have some skills there. Are any of them on a CD?"

"I have this CD here. It's nothing fancy which is both the name of it and what it is"

"How much?"

"Take one"

"No, I have to pay for it. You're not a great salesman, are you?"

"Nope, I guess not. Five bucks"

Tony handed over a twenty and said, "I'll take two".

"I said five, take four or if you can wait a couple of minutes, I will give you change"

"You need better marketing. Ten. I'll take two and we're even. Thanks"

"Thanks, I hope that you enjoy it. There's a line of sight warrantee"

"Whats a line of sight warrantee?" Tony asked.

"I thought you said you were a salesman? Not used cars, I guess. As soon as you are out of my line of sight, I am keeping your money" He chuckled.

Jessica was still cleaning up, so Tony went over to say goodby.

"That guy's pretty good"

"Yup, he is"

"Do you have his CD?"

"Nope"

"You do now" Tony handed her one of the two he bought.

"Thanks"

"See you soon"

"Yup"

Tony walked back to the Buick feeling a little lighter than when he went in and not just the twenty-five bucks he spent on tip and CDs lighter. It was early. Last call down at The Embers wasn't until one and it was barely eleven now. The Buick turned right out of the parking lot like it was one of those high-tech self driving cars they were talking about on NPR. It also knew to pull into the restaurant parking lot. Smart car. Tony got out and went in for a beer. Danny was working the bar, as usual. There was only a half dozen people in there.   Two guys were tossing darts over in the corner, one guy was shooting balls on what passed as a pool table, a couple at one of the small tables whispering to each other and giggling every few seconds and there was a woman sitting by the corner of the bar. Tony wasn't sure, but it may have been the "get something from my car" woman from the other night. His memory was a little foggy. He decided the best thing to do was sit as far away as possible, so he sat at the other end of the bar.

"Hey Danny, can I have a Bud Light?"

"Can you pay for it?"

"Yes, as a matter of fact I can. Have I ever stiffed you?"

"You're kidding, right?"

Tony did not remember ever stiffing Danny but that probably did not mean much. He threw a ten down on the bar. Danny brought him his Bud Light and dropped the change on the bar. Tony slid a buck over to the edge of the bar.

"Don't you ever drink anything but Bud Light?"

"The other night I had rum and coke"

"Oh yeah, big spender. Were have you been?"

Tony told him about the coffee shop, Jessica and the guy from Pennsylvania with the tenor guitar.

"I think Jessica used to waitress in the restaurant. I would need to ask Skip"

"Why don't you have live music here?"

"Skip doesn't want to pay the BMI and ASCAP fees. He also doesn't want to pay the musicians. He doesn't see any value in it."

"There are six people here and there were about forty or fifty in the coffee shop" Tony replied.

"Really?"

"Really"

The guy playing pool came over to the bar for a refill.

He put his glass down on the bar with a loud thud. "Jack"

"You think you might have had enough?" Danny asked though it was more a statement than a question.

"I'll let you know when I have had enough." pool table guy might be a mean drunk. "When are you going to fix this pool table? Half the felt on the bumpers is ripped and I don't think it is even flat"

"Is it not flat or are you a little tilted?" Danny laughed at his own joke. The pool table guy started to stand up straight as he could and glared for a little bit at Danny. His face was getting red and Tony thought he saw a little bit of spittle rolling down his cheek. Tony could see Danny reaching under the bar for his "calming stick". The calming stick was a two-foot piece of broom handle. Tony saw the stick and suddenly had the urge to get a cannoli. The stick wasn't out from under that bar yet and the pool table guy started laughing too.

"You know, you may be right" He said. As quickly as the storm blew in it was over. Danny gave pool table guy his drink and let him know that it should be his last one that night and he will get him an Uber. Pool table guy said "Don't worry, I don't have a car. I walk".

Danny wasn't always a bartender. Out of high school he enlisted in the Marines and did a tour in Iraq. He was going to make the Marines a career. After a year in the desert he changed his mind. He got out when his hitch was over and went to trade school to become a mechanic. He didn't talk about the marines much and always changed the channel when the news was on. He took the bartender gig as a second job to help to save some money for a house for his family. He wasn't a trained bartender but when all your customers either drank beer or shots you could get away with not knowing any of the fancy drinks. There was a book if he had to look something up. After all this time he still never needed the book.

"That was close" Tony said.

"Not even, I could tell he was going to back down. Some guys are pretty macho when they've had a few. He is a good guy deep down. Also, he is smart enough to back away from a six-foot marine holding a stick"

"You're not in the service any more"

"Once a marine always a marine"

"Remind me not to tick you off"

"You won't need reminding"

Tony drank his Bud light. Danny asked if he wanted a refill.

"You know, for some reason I don't feel like it." Tony replied.

Tony looked around the bar. The two guys were still playing darts. He noticed the woman at the end of the bar was gone. He didn't even see her leave. The pool table guy was sitting at one of the round tables with his head in his hands. He looked ready to pass out in the little bowl of pretzels. "I bet this place hasn't changed since nineteen sixty-three" he thought. The walls were paneled in dark faux mahogany panelling from the floor about halfway up. The top half of the walls were painted red. The chairs were covered in red naugahyde. There was a dart board, but the little chalk board used to keep score was so worn out as to be useless. The one pool table was pretty worn out as well. The green felt was shiny were the balls were usually racked and some of the felt over the bumpers was worn completely off. The coolest thing in the place was the old juke box.

"It's funny I have never noticed how tired this place was" He said.

Danny replied "You just seeing that now? Skip doesn't put a dime into this place"

Tony drove by the coffee shop on his way back home. The lights were all out. He supposed Jessica must be tucked in with the kids by now.

CHAPTER 10

MADISON MAKES VEGGIE LASAGNA.

Tony asked, "Do you remember where we put my boxes of school papers?"

Madison looks puzzled.

"What do you need those for"

"I told Mike and Guido I had case studies showing that efficiency does not always mean fewer workers, that often the work grows to fit the resources"

"Sounds like you were B.S.ing them"

"I hope not, they called my bluff. I am pretty sure we studied something to that affect though"

"Look in the attic"

The apartment they lived in was in an old Victorian house. The house had long lost its splendor and was now rudely divided into four apartments. Tony and Madison lived on the second floor and had access to the attic. The owner built some small storage places in the attic that his tenants used. Tony hated going up there because it was hot, dusty and there were spiders. He did not care for spiders.

He went up there anyway and found his box labelled "school- 1" in the little storage area and dragged it out to the aisle. The top was all dusty and he thought he saw mouse crap on it. "Great, I don't have rubber gloves" he thought. Tony was a little germaphobic. He went back downstairs and got a dust mask, some paper towels and rubber gloves and returned to the attic. After brushing the dust and poo off of the box cover, he opened it up. He did not bother to organize any of this stuff when he put it away. In fact, he never really expected to look at it again and was't sure why he even held on to it. Tony pulled every paper out and looked at it. None of them were what he was looking for. One paper looked out of place. It was hand written on yellow ruled paper in blue ink. Tony took it out and read it.

"Dear Tony" it was a letter from Madison. While he was studying for his MBA, she was away in Africa working for a non-profit. Tony did not understand working for free. He had to scrimp and save to go to school. Often, he worked nights and went to school during the day. Madison was from a different world and did not need to worry about paying for school or expenses. She had a trust fund.

"I wish you could be here with me. These kids are amazing! Today we studied arithmetic, or "maths" as they called it. I want to make this my life's work. There is so much we could do for these kids. They don't even have running water in their houses". Tony loved that she wanted to change the world. The rest of the letter made Tony blush. He folded it up and stuffed it in his pocket.

This box did not have what he was looking for. He grabbed one of the others, de-pooed it and dumped everything out. Aha! There it was "A study in productivity changes and resource allocation taking into account new automation in the insurance industry" It was real, maybe he wasn't BS-ing after all. Tony put everything back an went downstairs with his treasure.

"Found it!"

"That's great, Found what?" Madison was busy in the kitchen.

"The paper I was looking for"

"I knew you would. You never throw anything away"

"Is that a complaint?"

"No dear" Madison smiled and kissed Tony on the nose.

"Dinner is ready"

"Cool, what are we having?"

"Vegetarian lasagna"

Tony bit the inside of his cheek. Madison thought she could make lasagna. She couldn't. Not like his mom at least. First off lasagna was not vegetarian. It needed meat sauce. It needed real cheese. Madison made her lasagna with low fat cheese and sauce from a jar. Not like Tony's mom. He loved Madison, but she was not a cook. She was always trying to make him eat healthy.

"Thanks for making this" Tony actually did mean that.

"You missed the last two dinners home and I wanted to make you something good. You've been staying at work a lot"

"I know, I'm sorry. I'm the new guy and I need to make a good name for myself. I want to be successful"

"Money isn't everything"

"Easy for you to say- when you grow up without it, it looks pretty important"

"Just saying, there is more to life than work."

"I'm doing this for us"

They sat down and ate dinner in silence. After cleaning up the dishes Tony said "I'm going into the study to read up on this paper"

Madison went to the living room and flipped on the TV. She adored Tony for his work ethic and thought he was pretty smart. She appreciated that he wanted the best for her and, someday, for their family. Still, the living room was lonely.

Tony took the paper into work with him the next day and started sketching up a slide deck. He hoped to have something he could have Guido and Mike review that day so that he could get the publications people to make him a nice professional presentation. By the time he was done he had twenty slides made up.

"Guido, do you think we can go over these slides later?"

"You have something already?"

"Yup"

"Busy beaver, let me see"

"This is interesting, but can you get it down to four or five slides? You'll put people to sleep with this many. Remember these guys are usually a couple of cocktails into it before we make the pitch"

"Four or five? They won't get the full picture." Tony wasn't sure he could do it.

"They're usually not detail guys. Show them the ten-thousand-foot view and have the back up data in your back pocket. They really only care about 'how does this make me money' anyway"

Tony went back to his cube and laid all the slides out on the floor. He stood staring at them and trying to visualize how he could boil this all down.

"What happened, did an acetate tree explode in here?" Bob wandered over.

"Nope, just working"

"Working on what- you have a lot of slides there. What's that graph? Are we selling graphing programs now?"

"No. it's data on productivity versus efficiency." then in his mind "Something you clearly don't understand". Tony had not really warmed up to Bob. Bob seemed to spend too much time chatting and goofing around for Tony. Whenever there was a hallway bull session you could guarantee Bob would be there.

"Well, if you can't dazzle them with brilliance baffle them with B.S." Bob was full of these insightful sayings. Tony's least favorite one was "Common sense isn't common knowledge".

"I have to get to work. I need to finish this by tonight". Basically, a lie. Tony did not have a hard deadline.

"I was playing D & D last night with some guys form the programming group...."

"I need to get this done"

"I just played a wizard card and rolled the dice....."

"Can you move over I need little more space"

"Lenny though he had a dragon, but he didn't........"

"Look, Bob I don't know and don't care from nothing about D&D- I need to get this done!" Tony was losing it at this point.

"Oh, sorry- you should have said so" Bob's brain did not have the filter required to recognize irritation in another human being, so he walked away happy. Tony waited for his pulse to slow down and went back to work.

Finally, after about four hours of messing with it Tony had four slides that would do the trick. He reviewed them with Guido and they both took them to Mike. Mike approved, and Tony was allowed to go to publications to get them drawn up.

Publications was run by a very nice man called Charlie. He had group of writers and artists working for him. Tony gave him copies of the four slides. Charlie looked them over one by one.

"I can get them to you Tuesday"

"That's great, thanks"

"What's your extension if we have any questions?"

"It's on the drafts"

"So, it is, so it is. Tuesday"

Tony went back to his desk feeling pretty good. He seemed to be getting Mike and Guido's approval and they were happy with his work. This deserves a drink.

Tony felt bad about how he treated Bob earlier and was feeling just good enough about himself to be charitable, Bob would get a pity invitation.

"Hey Bob, let's grab that beer we talked about"

"Sure, let me call home first"

Bob called home and got permission to go out for a beer or two with Tony. Tony called home and arranged to miss dinner again.

There was a Ground Round near the office. Bob and Tony decided on that. Bob liked their burgers. They got a table. Bob ordered a big juicy burger. Tony ordered a Heineken on draft and no burger.

"So, Bob, I know you like D&D but what else do you do for fun"

"Golf. I like to golf"

"Do you golf near here?"

"The company owns a course in Groton. I go there a lot. My handicap is ten" Ten was pretty good. Tony was impressed. He did not know golf very well. "At least it was a sport and not a wussy card game", he thought.

"I've been thinking about taking up golf". Tony figured all successful business guys need to play golf.

"You can get lessons. As a sport it is very frustrating. It will let you do well just often enough that you don't want to quit." Bob said.

The conversation went from Golf to Red Sox to computers. Bob just bought an Apple two. Back to golf, avoided politics and religion and ended up on physics. Bob had a physics degree. He was more interesting than Tony first thought he was. Or maybe it was just the beer. Bob had a few. Tony stuck to one, He didn't want to be on the couch again.

Madison met Tony at the door with a big kiss. She saved him some dinner on a plate in the fridge. She made him chicken. It wasn't bad.

"How was Bob?" Madison asked,

"Better than I expected. I really lit in to him earlier in the day and felt kind of bad about it. I don't think that he noticed. He doesn't have that filter. How was your day?"

"Fine. I met the new neighbors, they have a dog. It's cute. It's a Lhasa."

"You mean 'yappy dog'"

"It didn't seem that yappy"

"What else did you do?"

"I put on a job application at the bank"

"I thought we decided you didn't have to work?"

"You decided, I want to work. I am bored. It's just a teller job, not much pressure"

She named the bank and it turned out to be the one Tony pitched the product to.

"A long as you're happy"

"I need to be busier" Madison replied.

Tony was raised in the old-world traditions and did not believe a wife should work, except around the house. His mother never worked. It is hard to undo twenty years of brain washing. He was trying really hard to be more of a late twentieth century man. In his mind he knew it was the right thing, his heart strongly disagreed. He did not like the idea of Madison working it made him feel like he couldn't provide. He knew Madison wanted to work and she would love to work in something with some social relevance but was willing to compromise for Tony's career. He really appreciated this about her.

CHAPTER 11

TONY LEARNS ABOUT SELLING MUSIC

Tony listened to the CD he bought from the old guy at the coffee shop. "This is some pretty good stuff" he thought. "How can some one be that good and be playing for tips at a coffee shop?". Tony clearly did not know the music business. It took more than good to succeed. Tony decided this guy needed marketing and he was just the guy to do it for him. He did not know from nothing how to do it, but he was a pro at one time. How hard could it be? The cd jacket had a contact email, so Tony dashed off a quick email.

"Hi Tom. My name is Tony Sincero. I heard you playing last week at the coffee shop near me. Remember I bought two CDs? Your music is fantastic. I think you could be big. I want you to let me do some marketing for you. I used to be a professional. Right now, I am between positions and have some free time"

Tom answered the email about a day later with a terse "I'm not interested". Tony was not going to take no for an answer. He wrote him back and gave him his phone number with an upper case "CALL ME". Tom was retired so he had some time. Tony sounded like a lunatic, but he lived far away, and they may never meet again anyway. He called the number.

"Tony speaking"

"Hello Tony, this is Tom from Pennsylvania. You wanted me to call"

"Yes, I did, thanks for getting back to me. I really enjoy your music and I think we can do something great together. I have a background in sales and marketing, I could help you a lot"

"That's nice, Tony" Tom was more than a little skeptical "Nobody wants to buy this music and I am too old in any case."

"How do you know if you don't try?" Tony asked.

"I tried, believe me. I tried. I was in several bands back in the sixties that just missed the big bus. I don't need that aggravation any more. I do this for fun and to hang with my friends"

Tony was persistent "I can do something for you. Let me try"

"What will it cost me?"

"Nothing"

"Nothing costs nothing. What's in it for you?"

"I crashed out of the sales game. Maybe if I can put this together, I can make a new career."

Tom was silent for about 30 seconds. "I'm not sure…"

"Trust me"

"The last guy that said 'trust me' still owes me money"

"I'm not that guy"

"Says you"

"Let me try, I need this" Tony was almost begging.

"Okay but I'm not sending you any money"

"No money"

Tony got Tom's phone number and a few details. "Okay, now what do I do?" he said to himself out loud. He was alone, so it did not matter. He decided to do the first thing he always did in these situations. Grab a beer and sit outside. A beer turned to three as he sat in his folding chair under the awning of his trailer. He had no ideas but was feeling pretty good.

Lorraine yelled out the window "What are you doing?"

"Thinking"

"You're slurring already because you said 'drinking' and it sounded like 'thinking'"

"I am thinking."

"Don't hurt yourself. Who's that singing? It doesn't sound like the usual girly bar crap you like to play."

"That's not girly bar music, it's country blues. We've been over that. This music is a guy from Pennsylvania I met the other night."

"Nice voice. He sounds like he must be about thirty. He's telling a story"

"All his songs pretty much are stories. Surprisingly enough he's looking at thirty a long way back on the rear view"

"I like it. I like stories"

"Would you buy this music?" Tony asked.

"It's not free?" Lorraine responded.

"Why should it be free?"

"Everything is free on the inter webs"

"Don't you think people should be paid for their work?"

"Not if it's free"

Tony could tell he was losing that one. This marketing thing may be harder than he thought. He opened another beer.

"When was the last time you bought music?"

"When it was on eight track. I only listen to the radio and the internet"

Tony didn't have a computer, so he didn't know much about listening to music on the internet. When he needed a computer, he went to the library. The library computers were good enough.

"Do you have a CD player?"

"I do, it's in the kitchen I think"

All those years in tech and Tony still became out of touch with the main stream world. Tony needed to know more about how people got their music if he was going to make this work. He headed to the coffee shop. Jessica was not there. It wasn't very busy so the girl with the lip rings and neck tattoo had nothing to do but talk to him. He asked her about how she got her music.

"Do you buy CDs?"

"Buy what?" She looked at him like he just said he could fly.

"CD's, you know those little round shinny records"

"I know what CD's are, I just don't buy any. I also know what records are. My friend Jason buys vinyl. They are cool. They are about this big around". She holds her hands about two feet apart. "You need a special table thing to play them. Jason says it's "analog" and sounds so much better. It sounds scratchy to me. He goes to some special stores to buy the disks."

"What do you do?"

"I stream music on my phone using an app called "Spotify". It doesn't cost nothing"

"Do you buy songs?"

" Naw, sometimes my friends copy them for me but mostly I stream them"

"Do you go to concerts?"

"Sometimes. I like the big shows at the football stadium with the lasers and smoke bombs and stuff"

"Do you like the music they have here at the coffee shop?"

"It's nice enough for old geezer's stuff. I need the whole show with the lights and dancing and fire works. All the cool stuff"

Clearly, she was not the target audience. Tony thanked her and headed out the door. It was early, too early for the bar, so he went to the library to look up "Spotify".

The library wasn't far from the coffee shop. This town wasn't that big. The librarian nodded his way when he came in. She recognized him but did not know his name. To her he was one of the steady stream of job seekers that came in to use the computers to search the internet and check on their LinkedIn profiles. The library held a class once a month to show people how to use the web to look for jobs. Everyone made a LinkedIn profile. Most of the people that came in for books looked happy. The job seekers always looked just a little beaten down. The job seekers were serious about what they did.

Tony nodded back at the librarian and took a seat behind one of the computers. He typed "Spotify" into the search box. Sure enough he could down load it and play all kinds of stuff. "I wonder what they pay the musicians" he thought. He would have to find that out. He typed "What does Spotify pay artists" into the little search block. The answer came back "the average "per stream" payout to rights holders lands somewhere between $0.006 and $0.0084". Well, not going to make Tom any money that way. If Tom got streamed a million times, he could make six grand. That's not going to put much baklava on the table. There was no way he could think to get Tom's music out to ten thousand people never mind a million or ten million. He might have bitten off more than he could chew with this project.

While he was at the library, he decided to check his LinkedIn profile. He had a few messages in his inbox. Three people added a skill and wanted him to endorse them for it. He laughed to himself. His endorsement was going mean both diddly and squat. There was a message from a former coworker who knew he was out of work and was offering a work from home position. He wanted to do him a huge favor. Tony didn't hardly know this guy, but the guy wanted to do him a huge favor anyway. The job involved selling some sort of diet supplement and getting other people to also sell it. What a great deal, the more people below him the more money he made. All he had to do was get five people to sign up under him and if they in turn got five people each to sign up under them and then they got five people each to sign up under them etc. Tony did the math and figured that after about 12 or so levels of this everyone in the world would be a sales rep and there would be no one left to buy the stuff. Ponzi had nothing on these guys. The last message was from the same guy that left his card. Tony read it and sat staring at the screen for five or ten minutes. He deleted the message and walked away from the computer.

"Have a nice day"

Tony thanked the librarian and went back to his car. Not too early for that drink now. He drove to The Embers.

CHAPTER 12

MADISON GOES TO WORK.

Madison worked in a little branch office of the bigger bank. The employees jokingly called it "bank in a box". They had a drive-up window with two places for cars and a lobby window for walk ins and not much else. Her job was to stand at the drive-up window and interact with the customers. Most of the customers were in a hurry so did not say much. They put their paper work in the little vacuum tube thing and sent to to her. Her coworkers were nice people. The branch manager was a thirty something year old woman who had been with the bank for ten years. Most of the branch managers were women. Pretty much all of the higher up managers were men. Some of the women had more qualifications than the men but they were women and it was a bank.

"You've been with the bank ten years?" Madison asked her manager.

"Yes, there wasn't much around when I graduated college. it was a recession. I took a job here to pay off the loans"

"Where did you go to school?"

"I did my undergrad at U. Mass and my MBA at B.U. I saw on your application you went to Smith" the manager said.

"I did"

"Why didn't you go on to grad school? Your grades were impressive"

"I got married"

"There's still time"

"I am supporting my husband's career. He needs me to work" he didn't really need her to work but that is what people expected to hear so she said it.

"That's fine but you need to take care of yourself. A woman needs to be independent these days. You can't rely on a man"

"Tony's reliable. He works hard"

"That's what they want you to think. You need to look out for you"

Right then a customer pulled up to the drive through. He rolled down his window and took the little cylinder out of its holder. He put his paper work in a sent it on its way to Madison. Madison took the cylinder out of the vacuum tube and typed the account number into the computer. The customer was depositing a pay check. Madison usually only notes the account number on the slips. Hardly ever does she notice the customer's name longer than to say, "Thank you Mr. so and so". This time the name looked familiar. It might be the Bob Tony spoke about. The paycheck was from the right company. He wasn't as nerdy looking as Tony described. Bob didn't look all that nerdy. He was a bit over weight. Okay, a lot over weight and needed a shave. No pocket protector and tape on his glasses as Tony described. It didn't matter. She wasn't going to strike up a conversation with him. It was too hard over the intercom and there were three more cars in line. She sent his receipts and cash back to him through the tube and said, "Thank you". He said, "Thank you" and drove off. Madison waited on the next three cars. One guy had three rolls of quarters he wanted to change to bills. The next guy had a paycheck to deposit and wanted twenty bucks back in cash.

"Can I get that twenty in three fives and five ones please sweetie?"

She was not his sweetie.

"Yes, You may." She answered as politely as possible.

He had fake dyed hair and was wearing a gold chain. It wasn't too hard to see from the bank window. He was driving an Eldorado and the top was down.

"You're cute, when do you get off work toots?"

He had an obvious tan line ring on his wedding ring finger. She was not his 'toots".

"Here's your twenty dollars, have a nice day" Madison replied politely.

"Don't be so serious honey"

She was not his honey.

"Thank you for your business"

"C'mon, be a sport- when do you get off work?"

"Sir you have to move on, we have other customers"- she held up her left hand to show her wedding ring.

He mumbled something about being a stuck up something or another and peeled out as he left.

"Don't let that bother you, we get those now and then". Her boss was watching.

"What do you do?"

"We do just what you did. You handled that perfectly"

"What if he comes back?"

"They never do"

The rest of Madison's day went pretty smoothly. At the end of the day they had to count the drawer and reconcile all the accounting for the night auditor. This night it went pretty late, one drawer was three cents over and they had to find the mistake. When Madison was leaving the Eldorado parked across the street with it's lights out. There was the shadow of someone behind the wheel.   She got into her car and locked all the doors for the drive home. All the way home she kept watching in her rear-view mirror to see if she was being followed. She didn't see anyone back there.

When Madison got home, Tony was already there. He wanted to make up for being a jerk about her job, so he had dinner all prepared. He didn't cook it. He brought home take out. It was the thought that counted. He asked her about her day.

"How was it?"

"Great, everyone was nice. I think your friend Bob deposited his pay check at the drive through"

"Oh yeah, how much does he make?"

'You know I can't talk about that" she smiled and giggled just a little. Tony liked the smile.

"Some skanky guy in an Eldorado tried to get me to out for drinks with him. He was disgusting and very rude"

"What did you do?"

"What could I do? I did my job and was polite. My boss said it happens now and then"

"You didn't tell him to get lost? That you were married? Did you get his name? Maybe I should talk to him" Tony was jealous.

"Calm down Rocky, it's just something we all have to deal with. It goes with the territory"

"Not this territory, I'll kick his ass" Tony was old world about these things.

"No, you won't. He won't even ever be back at the bank, probably" The rational part of her brain was outraged at Tony's display of cave man bravado but somewhere deep in the lizard part of her brain she was feeling protected. Tony poured her a wine and sat at the kitchen table.

"My training period is almost over. I am going to get a territory assigned soon, it might mean moving."

"I just got this place straightened out and started a job." Madison protested.

"Hey, you knew this might happen. It's only a teller job and this place is rented month to month. We can move anytime"

It was only a teller job, but it was her teller job.

The rest of the dinner was silent. Tony read the paper and Madison cleaned up the dishes.

The phone rang.

"Would you get that, I'm reading the paper"

"Okay fine". Fine was never fine. It turned out to be for her. It was the police.

"Is this Madison Sincero?" a husky voice on the other end of the line asked.

"Yes, it is, what can I do for you?"

"This is sergeant Roland. Do you know a man named Richard Lesman?"

"I cannot say that I do. What's this about?"

"Mr Lesman was parked outside of your house and the neighbors got nervous and called us. He claims that he was waiting for you and that you expected him"

"I don't even know who he is" She was getting nervous now.

Right then Tony yelled over "Who are you talking to?"

"It's the police. They have some guy that was parked outside the house waiting for me. He claims to be a friend and I don't know the name"

"I bet it's that guy from before, Are they outside? I'll kick his ass." Madison counted up how many glasses of wine they had.

"You shouldn't go out there, you've had too much wine and I don't know what you had before you left work"

"I'm fine, I'm going out there" Tony put on his shoes. Madison realized he was tipsier than she thought when he almost fell over picking up his shoes.

"Stay in here" she was adamant now.

"No!" He was full on gorilla.

Tony stomped out of the front door and saw a police car across the street. They were standing and talking to a man who fit the description Madison gave him earlier of the skanky guy. He decided that he had to defend his wife and started over there. He tripped on a garden hose an picked himself back up. The embarrassment just made him angrier.

"Whoa buddy, stop right there, who are you?" The policeman held up his left hand in a "halt" kind of position. His right hand was touching his billy club. The other police man was watching the man they were questioning.

"Never mind who I am. That man threatened my wife"

"Calm down, let's sort this out"

"I'm calm, Let me at him"

The police man grabbed Tony's arm and locked out his elbow. "Do I need to restrain you? You are very close to a drunk and disorderly charge. Don't add assault to that"

"This man was at my wife's work today and threatened her"

"Is that true sir?" The cop directed his question to the other man.

"I don't know this guy; how do I know his wife?"

"You jerk, you were at the bank today and you got belligerent when my wife would not agree to go out with you" Tony's words were staccato.

"That stuck up bitch was your wife? You are playing above your level boy" He'd been drinking.

"So, you admit it?"

"I don't admit squat"

"If I let go of you will you behave?" the policeman asked Tony.

By now Tony had calmed down quite a bit. "Yes". The policeman let go of Tony's arm

"Let's get to the bottom of this"

By now Madison put on some shoes and came out to the street.

"Ma'am, do you know this man?" She wasn't sure in the dark, but she thought he may have been the man from the bank.

"I am not sure"

"Sure, you know me sweetie, I was at your bank today" Once he spoke, she was sure she recognized him.

"He was at the drive up at the bank today. He tried to ask me out and I ignored him"

"She's stuck up"

"Sir, why are you parked out here?"

"It's a free country." was the man's only response.

"Did you follow this woman home?"

"What if I did?"

"That's harassment. I'm taking you in for being drunk and disorderly and this woman is free to come to the station and charge you with harassment "

The policemen handcuffed the man and put him in the back of the cruiser. They called the station to get his car towed out of there.

"Would you like to come down to the station and press charges?"

"Not really, I just want him to leave us alone"

"Let me come down there and kick his ass". Tony was still a little angry.

"We can't do that sir, and, in your condition, I advise you to not leave this property and please do not drive or we'll be taking you in too"

The other policeman handed her a business card "If you have any more problems with him please call this number right away."

Madison took the card and thanked the officer.

"You're quitting that job!" Tony was red faced.

"No, I am not"

"Yes, you are! I am not having strange men stalking my wife"

"You're making too big a thing about this. Lighten up"

Tony wasn't going to "lighten up". He poured himself a whiskey and sat down in the living room staring at the front door. He was angry. Madison went closed herself in her room. Tony spent the whole night sitting and staring. This night he didn't even sleep on the couch.

Madison was a bank teller. Her feminist literature major prepared her for this. That was her running joke. She actually majored in economics. She did do a minor in literature though. Her family had money and she was raised to be well rounded. Her parents were not too enthusiastic about her marrying a guy from a working-class back ground who was so crass as to be a career sales man. They paid for her to go to the best schools, Groton, Smith. They expected her to marry into a wealthy family and be part of polite society. They certainly did not expect her to work at such a menial job.

"You mean you touch other people's money?" Her mother was incredulous.

"Yes, I have to count it and put it in the drawer."

"Why do you want to do this?"

"I need something to do during the day. Tony works long days and sometimes into the night and I am bored"

"Join a country club dear. They have lady's tea and ladies tee times. You can meet good people" Her mother replied.

"Idle people who have nothing better to do. I want to meet real people. Besides, we can't afford it right now" Madison said.

"You can afford it, you have your trust."

"We are not living off of that. Tony wants us to pay our own way"

"That's ridiculous. You are never going to have a comfortable life relying on his work. He is not that kind of guy. His parents don't even speak English. You come from better stock"

"This is what I have chosen to do mother"

"Now you're just rebelling. Come home where you belong"

"I'm married mother"

"We have lawyers. Your uncle knows the best ones in DC. We can fix this, and you won't lose a dime"

"I love him mother. I don't want to come home"

"Suit yourself, the door is always open, we kept your room the way you left it."

Madison hung up the phone. "That went well" she mumbled.

CHAPTER 13

TONY GOES OUT WITH JESSICA

The phone rang. "Who is that" he wondered. "No one ever calls me." Tony had toyed with cancelling his phone entirely. You need a phone though if you are going to be a serious job seeker.

"Hello"

"Hi Tony, it's Jessica. Jessica from the coffee shop"

Tony knew who she was. He only kew the one Jessica. "How are you doing?"

"I am not bad" He told her.

"I hope I am not too forward. You seemed to like the music at the coffee shop and, well, that is, I have two tickets to Passim for Saturday night. I don't know if you know Passim…" Tony knew Passim well. "There is a guy called David Francey playing there, He's from Scotland by way of Canada. He's won Juno awards"

"Are you asking me to go with you?"

"I got a sitter and I would hate to waste a sitter and a ticket. My girlfriend can't make it. Sorry about the short notice"

"I would love to go. Where should I pick you up?"

"I'll meet you at the coffee shop- six o'clock. We can eat at the place"

"Good, see you there"

Tony didn't know if this was a date or two friends going to see music. He decided to be conservative about it. He didn't bring candy or flowers. Tony offered to drive.

"Do you know how to get to the square?" Jessica asked.

"I do"

They got into Tony's Buick and headed down route 3. It was a nice night.

"I know some places we can park on the street for free if you don't mind a little walking"

"I don't mind, I wore my city shoes" She said.

"City shoes, what are city shoes"

"They are my shoes for walking on pavement. City shoes. You don't have city shoes?"

"I have two pairs of shoes. These…" He held up his foot for her to see his shoes. They were old running shoes. A little worn out but they did not have any holes. "and my interview shoes which I only wear to interviews, weddings and funerals. I hope they still fit me. I have not needed them in a while"

"Interesting"

"What kind of work do you do?"

"I was a spy for the NSA. I worked all over Europe during the cold war."

"Just like James Bond?"

"Yup, just like James Bond but cooler". Tony was lying through his teeth a surprised Jessica believed him.

"Did you have a gun and a fancy car?"

"Yup, A Ruger and an Astin Martin DB9"

"Did you have a license to kill? Did you always get the pretty girl, and did she have a double entendre name?" She was on to him.

"Yes, I did always get the girl"

"Now I know you are lying. What did you really do?"

"I sold computer software. Not so exciting eh?"

"My ex husband was an auto mechanic"

"That's honest work. It benefits society. Selling is dirty"

"The work was honest; the embezzling and womanizing was less than honest. He thought he was hot stuff in that Caddy he drove. My parents warned me about marrying a man that much older than me" She said.

"Sorry to hear that"

"Don't be sorry, I got my daughter out of the deal and someday, when she is well, we will be a family. At least for now I still have the grand kids"

"That's nice"

"How about you? What about your grand kids?"

"Things didn't go so well with me. My daughter and the kids moved to Ohio to be closer to her mother. None of them are really talking to me." Tony was surprised at himself. That is not a subject area he likes to go to.

"Maybe someday you will be able to see them?"

"I can only hope. They say that I need to get my act together" Tony was already saying more than he wanted to.

Tony found a place to park off the square. It was his lucky day. The night air was pleasant, and they had a very nice walk together over to Palmer street. They talked about music, the Sox, the weather- everything but family. Tony felt good that he was able to talk as much as he did in the car about family with out breaking down. He didn't want to speak any more about it. He knew his problems could be his own fault.

The nice woman at the door looked up Jessica's reservation. They had seats at table fifteen. Tony and Jessica went in and took their seats.

"Have you seen David before?" Jessica asked.

"I haven't. Thanks for inviting me. How much do you want for the ticket"?

"You're buying dinner" Jessica smiled

"Fair enough".

The waitress came by with the menus and took their drink order. Tony decided to behave and ordered a root beer. Jessica look puzzled for second and ordered soda and lime.

"When was the last time you were here?"

"I came last summer to see Cliff Eberhardt"

"Cool, I love him. He's one of my favorites"

"He is the real deal." Tony knew good writing when he heard it. He didn't know why it was good, but he knew what he liked.

"They used to only have veggie food here"

"This is a new menu" Jessica was not a vegetarian.

The concert was great. Tony had a new favorite to add to his list.

Tony dropped Jessica back at her car at coffee shop. For an awkward minute they stood by the car and stared at each other. Tony reached out and grabbed her hand to shake good night. Jessica pulled him close and kissed him square on the mouth. Tony started to kiss back then suddenly pulled back.

"What's wrong?" Jessica said

"I have to go I will see you soon? "

"Sure" Jessica sounded puzzled and maybe a little hurt.

Tony shook her hands again and got back in his car.

"See you later"

"Yup, bye"

Jessica walked to her car slowly, staring at her feet.

Tony drove back to his trailer and parked in his usual spot. He sat for few minutes in the driver's seat and banged his palms repeatedly on the steering wheel. "Stupid, stupid Tony" he said to himself over and over again.

Chapter 14

Tony Gets A Chance to Shine

Alice watched a red eyed droopy shouldered Tony walk through the door and by her desk. He looked like something the cat wouldn't even bother to drag. The cat would probably just bury him in the yard if it could find enough sand.

"Holy crap- what happened to you?" Alice asked in almost a motherly tone.

"Long story, I didn't sleep much last night."

"Get cleaned up, slap some water on your face- you and Guido have a meeting with the bank guys at nine."

Darn, Tony forgot this. He dumped his stuff off in his cube and went to the men's room to clean up. He splashed some water on his face and straighten out his shirt.

"What happened to you?" Guido was standing by his cube.

"Allergies" Tony lied.

"Let's go, we have the bank guys coming in to review the bid."

The bank guys showed up on time, as usual. There was the gaggle of suits and, Tony was happy to see, Sandy. They all sat on one side of the long table in the exec conference room. The alpha banker, as Tony took to thinking of him, sat in the middle. He had a minion on either side. They both seemed to fall over each other agreeing with him. Sandy was sitting all the way to the left side of the table. Alice came in and handed everyone a binder with the product specs and a copy of the proposal. She took coffee orders and left the meeting. Tony noticed that publications had done a really nice job on the binders. There was an illustration on the cover of a woman sitting in front of a terminal and a man standing behind her looking over her shoulder. The man had his right hand on her shoulder and was slightly bent over. His left hand held a coffee cup. The man looked familiar to him. After a bit he realized that the man looked like him! The illustrators were known to sneak in little acorns, as they called them, Tony didn't know whether to be angry or flattered.

"We have reviewed your proposal" The Alpha banker spoke. "I think we need a few concessions. IBM was in last week and their product looks pretty interesting"

"Did they make a proposal?" Guido asked though he was sure they didn't. Their tactic was to sow F.U.D. Fear Uncertainty and Doubt. That has always been the strategy with smaller competitors then come in with a proposal at a higher dollar amount. Wang was not yet big enough that that would not work.

"They warned us that you may not be around for the long term"

"We are a public company. You've seen our annual reports. We've had fantastic growth and have money in the bank. What do you think?" Mike almost sounded snide.

The two minions on either side of the alpha banker whispered in his ear. The alpha banker held his hand up with the palm toward one of them.

"We are going to need some kind of guarantees before we bet our business on this"

"What is your biggest worry?" Guido asked.

Sandy spoke up "One concern is that our documents will be orphaned if you decide to drop this product and we will not be able to get to them". F.U.D. The minions looked slightly annoyed at Sandy. She was to be seen and not heard.

"We have that covered" Tony spoke up. "Any time you can save your documents in 'plain text' to an eight-inch floppy disk. IBM can read those disks and use those plain text files. You will only have to do some reformatting. I am sure we can create a translator to reformat the documents for you"

Guido gave Tony the "I hope you know what you are talking about" look.

The alpha banker asked if they could have the room for a few minutes. Tony, Guido and Mike left the conference room.

"Tony, I hope you know what you are doing. You just promised something we don't have" Guido whispered just in case they could hear him.

"Don't dig us a hole we can't get out of kid". Mike wanted to yell but also whispered.

"Don't worry. It's covered. Bob has been messing around with stuff and wrote a little program to change our formatting codes to IBM's formatting codes and back again. It's not production ready but it works. When we did the demo, Sandy wanted to use some of their documents and Bob helped".

"Bob, the wiring closet guy that never bathes?"- Mike asked incredulously.

"Bob the wire guy is a lot smarter than he lets on" Tony said.

The alpha banker gestured for them to come back into the room.

"We've discussed this. We will go with you if you will include the program to translate the documents"

"We may not have that ready right away, it will take three months"

"We want a guarantee."

"It will be in the final contract. We'll need an extra $20k to cover the expense" Tony spoke up.

"$10K" the alpha banker relied.

"$15k"

"Okay, I can live with fifteen. Put the deal together"

They all shook hands and left the meeting with a handshake deal. Tony would work with legal to draw up the contracts. Mike walked the bankers to the lobby. When he returned, he called Guido and Tony into his office.

"Nice work in there guys. How did you know he would pay for that extra software?"

"I spent a lot of time with Sandy when we demoed the new stuff for her. She let slip then that the alpha banker hated IBM. They screwed him over in a previous bank."

"So, why did he hesitate to go with us?"

"His board. I looked into his board. One of the guys is the son in law of an IBM vice president. The alpha was going to need a good answer for not going with IBM or this guy would make him miserable" Tony had done his research.

"So…"

"I conspired with Sandy to bring up the orphan document thing because I knew we could handle it and it gave him a win and reason to go our way"

"That's genius kid" Mike sounded happy.

Mike opened his top left desk drawer and pulled out a bottle. "Thirty-year-old Scotch. Older than you kid". He filled three glasses and they toasted their good fortune.

Mike bellowed "Alice! Get Bob in here"

Alice paged Bob. He showed up about ten minutes later.

"Bob, you wrote a program to translate formatting between IBM and us?" Mike asked

"And back, both ways, it's a hack though. The code is all sloppy" Bob added.

"What are you working on right now?"

"Cleaning up the wiring closet and adding the new VS2200"

"Can some one else do that?"

"We don't have any one else"

"Hire a guy. We need you to turn your program into something we can sell."

"What?"

"You have three months. Don't let me down" No one ever dared let Mike down.

"I will try my best" Bob replied, not sounding confident.

"You will DO your best". Mike always said this. Maybe he should have a sign made.

Tony went from goat to golden boy all in the space of the same deal. He couldn't wait to get home to tell Madison.

Bob showed up at Tony's cube a little after lunch. Tony could tell he had a couple of beers, but he wasn't too drunk.

"You jerk, you threw me under the bus!!!" Bob was a little irate.

"What do you mean? This is a chance for you to shine" Tony did not understand not being ambitious.

"Shine my ass. I have worked hard at keeping below the radar. Visibility can get you shot here"

"C'mon visibility is how you succeed and advance"

"What makes you think I want to advance? I am perfectly happy running wires and fixing stuff"

"You're better than that. You went to college. You know computers, I've seen your work. You are a good programmer"

"I also know that no good deed goes unpunished. I was happy when Mike did not know who I was"

"He knows who everyone is"

"Maybe but it was easier to live up to low expectations."

Tony never bothered to think about whether or not Bob wanted this pressure. In his mind everyone was as ambitious as he. He didn't think someone would be perfectly happy to be a small cog. He thought everyone had his eye on the next rung of the ladder.

Bob didn't want the pressure. He came to Wang after having started and lost his own company writing software for IBM main frames. He specialized in custom accounting programs. Bob was a software savant. He studied math in college and had a master's degree in something called "topology". Tony had no idea what that meant. While he was in grad school Bob was able to get time on the mainframe in the school's computer lab. That is where he found that he had a knack for programming and wrote a few programs to illustrate some of his theories for his thesis paper. He was then dating his soon to be, and now ex, wife at the time. She was a CPA at one of the big three accounting firms. She noticed that some of his techniques could apply to business accounting. She and Bob together wrote a program that tracked accounts in nearly real time. She showed to to her boss at the firm and he showed it to a venture capitalist. "Reliable Accounting Systems "was born. They were able to hire a small staff and work on the products. Bob's wife turned out to be very good at seeing what the accounting world would buy and Bob was good at creating the products. For the first year they worked 80-hour weeks. They barely slept and never went home. Bob lost thirty pounds that year. They were married during that year on a Sunday and were back in work on Monday. They would go on a honeymoon later. That first year they grossed 2 million dollars in sales. The second year they grossed ten million. The board made Bob's wife CEO and Bob was in charge of technology. By the third year they were so busy Bob now had thirty people in the development group. He was losing control of the designs and did not actually like it. He was known as a micro-manager; micro management was okay when the group was small but now was slowing things down. Bob didn't communicate, or delegate, well and kept a lot of stuff in his head. People would waste a lot of time trying to guess what Bob wanted. Several of Bob's underlings went to his wife to complain.

"We have a problem. Bob will not delegate and we are spinning our wheels waiting for direction or, when we do do something, he changes it if it is isn't the exact way, he would do it"

"Just talk to him, I don't have time for this"

"We have spoken to him. He is not changing. You have to do something about it, you're his boss"

"I am also his wife. What do you think that should I do?"

"Get him out if the way. Fire him. Ship him off. Just do something or we will walk."

The pressure of being CEO and working together had already put a wedge between Bob and his wife. This would be the final straw. She called him into the office and closed the door.

"You're firing me? This is my company!"

"Our company. I am not firing you just moving you to a different area"

"Yeah, 'individual contributor', special projects, future proofing. I know an ice floe when I see one."

"If you don't like it quit"

"I will quit! and I will get my stuff out of the house before you get home tonight" Bob slammed the door and stomped off. That was Bob's last bout with "visibility". He still owned part of the company and made a few dollars when the company was sold to IBM a couple years later. He took the job at Wang to keep busy and make a few extra dollars. He was perfectly happy being a low-level invisible working stiff. He did not need "visibility".

"You're signed up for it" Tony reminded him

"Thanks for nothing" Bob replied

Tony was home from work unusually early that day. Madison had not seen him that early in the day recently. It was a nice surprise.

"Is everything okay at work? You are home awfully early."

"Fantastic. We closed the bank deal. All I have to do is get Bob to write some software for their documents."

"That is great how did you pull that off?"

"Chutzpah, and knowing Bob pretty much already wrote the software"

"What did Bob think?"

"He wasn't too happy at first, but I think he's coming around. He said I threw him under the bus"

"Did you?"

"Kind of did. He has the chops but not the ambition. He will thank me later"

"Before or after he kills you?" Madison smiled.

"I'm starved, what's for dinner?"

"I didn't expect you home so .... nothing"

"Grab your coat- we are going out in that case. We are getting steaks and bourbon"

Tony was happy. This deal means big things for him. Madison grabbed her coat and put on her shoes. They went out to the steak house.

"Table for two- by the window if that is possible" Tony liked the table by the window.

"Right this way sir"

The maitreD' led Tony and Madison to a table by the window overlooking the pond. He handed them some menus and a wine list and said, "Your Waitress is Michelle, she will be right with you".

"Good evening, my name is Michelle. Can I start you off with some drinks?" Michelle came over to the table almost as soon as the MaitreD left.

"Bourbon"

"And you madam?"

"I will just have water, Thanks. Lemon and little ice"

"How many bourbons have you had today?" Madison asked Tony.

"This will be my first. It's been a busy day"

Madison was a little skeptical but nodded anyway.

"This is a big deal for you?"

"Yes, it is, this is the kind of deal that can make my reputation in the company. It will put us over quota this quarter and I brought it in"

"I am proud of you."

"Thank you"

Michelle came with the drinks and asked, "Do you care for any appetizers?"

"I think we are ready to order. I will have the prime rib, rare, with mashed potatoes and my wife will have the small sirloin done medium well"

"Do you want a salad?"

"Yes, blue cheese dressing"

"I will have french dressing" Madison spoke up.

"Very well, thank you"

"How dd you know I wanted sirloin?"

"You always get that"

"You didn't even ask, next time let me make my own order!"

Tony was so excited about his big deal that he slipped back into his old word attitude and didn't think to let Madison make her own order. He apologized.

"Sorry, old habits. Did you have a good day?"

"I had a pretty uneventful day. Thanks for asking"

"Anything new at the bank?"

"The president came by to check out the branch. They said every now and then he slums with the peons. He came through with his entourage of yes men and shook everyone's hand"

"I think I've met him. They came to the company for the presentation"

"He is not very impressive" Madison added. Tony knew that it took a a lot to impress Madison. The truth was the bank guy was not very impressive.

"You could run that bank"

"I am not you. "

"You could be, you could assert yourself. You are probably about the smartest person there." Tony was proud of how smart Madison was and did not understand why she did not want to push herself.

CHAPTER 15

No Regrets

A sun beam was coming through the kitchen window of his double wide and spotlighting the coffee cup on the table. It was a very cheerful scene that was totally lost on Tony. He sat staring at the coffee until it had gone cold. Then he stared some more. The day after he went to the concert with Jessica Tony was still mad at himself. He had blown it. He would be lucky of she ever spoke to him again. Tony poured the cold coffee down the drain and set about making some more. "What was I thinking?" He asked himself. He was in no mental condition to socialize. He had a long way to go. Jessica was such a very nice person and deserves better. Tony dumped the old coffee grounds into the trash. "I am a such an idiot" he thought. He filled the coffee basket with a new filter and new coffee. He liked Dunkin Donuts coffee and bought ground coffee there rather than at the store. "She will never speak to me again" he moaned to himself. He closed the basket on the coffee maker. "I am a moron" now he was chastising himself. He poured water into the coffee maker and turned it on. After a few minutes the coffee maker made the happy, bubbly noise that told Tony he was getting fresh coffee soon. He rinsed his coffee cup out and waited. The coffee maker always takes longer when you stand there holding an empty cup and stare at it, but Tony had nothing else to do. Finally, the coffee was ready. Tony poured himself a cup of coffee, added the cream and two sugars.

The phone started ringing. His cell phone had hundreds of ring tones and Tony preferred the one that actually sounded like a phone was ringing. He was old school that way. He did not want t to hear some cutesy ring tone. He did not want his phone to play "Rhapsody in Blue" when someone called. If he wanted to hear "rhapsody" he would play an actual recording. He liked bells just the way Alexander Graham meant it to be. "Where did I put that thing?" Tony mumbled. He missed the days of wired phones hanging on the wall in the kitchen. He always knew where that phone was., it was on the wall in the kitchen. The place wasn't that big, but it took more than three rings to find the phone. Somehow it had ended up under the dish towel in the kitchen. At least he found his keys too, they were in the same place. When he got home the previous night, he just threw everything on the counter in a fit of self loathing. The old wired phone never told who who called. It was Jessica. At least this phone, even though it was too stupid to be where he looks for it, was smart enough to tell him that much. Now he wondered what she wanted, and should he call back. Maybe she wanted to let him know all was okay or maybe she wanted him to apologize for wasting a baby sitter. Maybe even pay for the baby sitter. He paced back and forth. He finished his coffee and still hadn't made a decision. Well, he made one decision. He decided to go across the street to buy a paper and sit outside and read it. Maybe he could think while he read.

The store across the street was unique. It was actually two stores. One side was a liquor store that was closed on Sundays and the other side was a neighborhood convenience store. The cashier sat in a little room between to the two where he could service customers for each store. Tony didn't go in there very often, it was apparent that cleanliness and maintenance were not the first priorities and Tony was a little germaphobic. Most of the stuff in the store had dust on it and Tony saw that a lot of things were past their 'sell by' dates. "Like me" Tony chuckled. The cashier was sitting in his little booth watching the Three Stooges on a little black and white television when Tony came in. Tony wondered around the front area of the store looking for the newspapers. The cashier was laughing at the television.

"Haaa, haha these guys are freakin' nuts" he laughed at the Stooges "You looking for the paper?" he sounded like Popeye.

"I am, are you out?"

"I knew you were looking for the paper. I can tell. I'm what you might call observational. And no, I am not out- you have to go around the back past the frozen foods they're at the end of the aisle"

"Thanks"

Tony walked past shelves and shelves of canned goods and packaged foods all dusty and in disarray. Past the candy. Past the soda. Past the ice-cream freezer and finally to the far end of the store. There were the papers stacked against the freezer. He picked up today's Globe and hiked back to the cashier.

"If you don't mind me asking, what do you keep the paper there? Most stores have them by the cashier"

"That's because most stores are run by morons, if I put the paper back there you have to walk by everything in the store to get it. Maybe you will buy something else. Smart eh?"

"Yeah Popeye, you're a freakin' genius" Tony said sarcastically to himself. Out loud he said "Oh, okay"

"I could have been a diver for Jacques Cousteau you know"

"The TV guy, yeah right. pull the other one"

"No lie, slick. Before I went to Korea I worked for an egghead in Cambridge. We made underwater breathing stuff. He wanted me to go to sea with him"

"And you didn't?"

"Uncle Sam had other ideas."

"Bummer"

"I'm happy- hey look at that! That Moe is a pistol" He pointed a crooked, nicotine stained finger back at the TV and laughed until he coughed. "Yup, could have dove with Cousteau"

Tony took his paper, folded it under his arm, and went back across the street.

The air had a heavy feeling for so early in the day. Tony sat on his folding chair under his awning and stared straight ahead at nothing in particular. He wasn't even reading the paper he just bought across the street. Directly across from him was a big pine tree that had been there since before the park was built. He liked that tree. Tony liked old trees. He also noticed the neighbor across the way had a garden gnome. He hated garden gnomes. He liked trees, hated garden gnomes. Garden gnomes look smug to him with their folded arms and closed mouth smiles. This one had a little tiny picket fence in front of it like it was his own little gnome yard. Weeds grew up around it. He hated garden gnomes.

"Hey meat head" Lorraine was at the window. "Meat head" was a new one. She had never called him that before. "What are you doing out there? There's a storm coming"

"Are you sure? It's pretty sunny out right now"

"Not now, later, maybe day after tomorrow- don't you watch the news?"

"I haven't for a couple of days"

"Big storm heading up the east coast, biggest hurricane since Irene"

"That's what I need"

"Troubles? Did the chem trails get you? That CIA guy come back?"

"No, the chem trails did not get me and he was not a CIA guy. I took a woman out last night. I might have screwed up" Tony told Lorraine the whole story about the concert and Jessica and almost kissing her. Lorraine listened attentively. So attentive Tony was not sure she hadn't fallen asleep. She didn't.

"You are a bone head, are you sure the chem trails didn't get you? What is wrong with you?" "Bone head" another new name.

"I was asking myself that"

"You need to call that woman. I don't think it is as bad as you think it is."

"It was worse, you were not there."

"I don't need to be there. Believe it or not I am a woman. I know these things" Sparky barked. "See, even the dog agrees with me."

Lorraine had already been drinking that day and was sounding a little bit loud. Tony knew she was about to launch into an extended lecture and wanted to stop it but not get her angry with him.

"I don't know Lorraine, I think I blew it. I am not ready to jump into something right now"

Lorraine sighed. Tony thought he heard her take a big draught off of something. Her lecture wheels were spinning up. No stopping it now.

"You think you are the first guy to get dumped? You think you are the first guy to get cold feet with something new? Stop being so pitiful. Hoist your self up. If you are interested in this woman don't give up so easily. Did she tell you you screwed up? I don't think so"

"Maybe I am not interested"

"Oh yeah, then why are you moping around?"

"I don't know"

"You want to have a drink with me?"

"Not right now"

"You're moping. You are interested in her"

"No and I don't think so"

"Call her, you chucklehead." "Chucklehead?" Did she have some kind of insult thesaurus?

"Eh"

"Call her, don't be a jerk. And don't forget the storm is coming"

"uhuh"

Tony went back into his trailer and picked up his phone.

Back in the 'phone on the wall' days he would have to look up the number and dial it. He would have a built-in excuse. Maybe he couldn't find the number or didn't remember it. Maybe he could dial the coffee shop instead of her home number. Maybe he would call the home number and she wouldn't be there. There were a lot of outs in the old days. This was the future though. Everyone had cell phones and it seemed they always had them with them everywhere they went. He didn't even have to know the number he could just have his phone call back the number. Maybe he should listen to the message first. She left a message.

"Hi Tony, this is Jessica, but you probably know that from the phone. I had fun last night. I uh, I just wanted to see if you were okay. I hope you don't mind me calling. Anyway, I will see you later?"

She did not sound mad. Maybe he was overreacting. Did she want to see him later or was that just something people say? She did make it sound more like a question than a statement. He pushed the redial button on the phone. Then he quickly pushed the cancel button. Tony paced around the room. Looked out the window. Washed his coffee cup. Looked out the window again. Looked at his phone. Opened the fridge. There were five beers in there. he reached for one then put it back. He looked out the window again and back to his phone. He pushed the redial button.

"Hi Tony"

"How did you know it was me?, oh yeah, twenty first century"

"Are you okay? Sorry of I was too presumptuous last night"

"I am fine, you were fine. It's just...."

"You didn't have fun? "

"No, not that. I just am not sure....."

"Sure, if what?"

"Sure, I am ready to be close to anyone"

"That's fine, I understand"

"That last few years have been difficult. Mostly my own fault. I don't want to screw up again"

"No pressure Tony, take it slow. I am working tonight, come by if you can. I'll give you free coffee" Tony swore he could hear a smile in that voice.

"I may just do that; can I have a cookie too?"

"Don't push it" Tony definitely heard a smile that time.

"Okay, see you later"

Tony hung up the phone and stuffed it back into his pocket. Things didn't quite look as bad. Maybe Lorraine was right.

CHAPTER 16

BOB IS IN TROUBLE

"Hey Bob, how's that project going?" Tony yelled out to Bob as he walked by his cube. Bob was on his way back from the snack machine with a big bag of Doritos and a Coke.

"Okay, I guess" Bob mumbled.

"What do you mean you guess?"

"I am a little behind. It's taking longer than I thought"

"I see you leave at the crack of five everyday and I see you wonder in at nine thirty or ten. Can you stay late or get on early to work on it? We only have three more weeks"

"I am not that much of a morning person plus I have my bowling league on Wednesdays and a standing D&D game on Thursdays. I am pretty busy, there's not a lot of free time". This irritated Tony to no end, but he could not let it show. Bob clearly was not taking this as seriously as Tony had hoped. Clearly, he did not impress on Bob the 'bet your career' aspects of this assignment. Bob wouldn't care anyway. He didn't actual have a career. In his view he just had a job. Tony was the career bettor.

"Don't you think this may be a little more important than those things?"

"Are you paying me overtime?" Bob replied but Tony knew that Bob didn't really care about the money.

"You're salary, you don't get overtime. There is a bonus if you get done on time"

"Let em see what I can do" Bob ripped open his bag of Doritos and strolled away like he had no particular place to be.

"You do that." Tony was not even sure Bob heard him.

Tony walked away from the conversation with a hopeless feeling and a stomach load of doom. This was his first personnel challenge. Tony walked from one end of the building to the other and back about six times.

He thought back to all his school studies to try to figure out what he should do. His course load was light on interpersonal relationships. School mostly concentrated on things that could quantified like earnings, schedules and budgets. He couldn't threaten to have Bob fired. Bob didn't really need the money. He had cash in the bank and lived like a grad student. He seemed happy with an old car, small apartment and what vacations he could get on the cheap. Bob was not very materialistic. He couldn't be bought. He knew he couldn't threaten Bob with demotion or being passed over for promotion. Bob had no goals beyond being what he was. Tony had absolutely no leverage on Bob. For a brief instance he thought of threatening Bob physically but that passed quickly. Tony was not pugilistic, not when he was sober at least.

"What are you up to?" Guido saw Tony walking in the hall. Tony didn't know whether to mention Bob to Guido at all. Would it look like Tony can't handle a project? Would Guido have second thoughts about handing this over to him? Tony decided to risk it and seek advice.

"I am trying to figure out how to motivate Bob. He is falling behind"

"That is a tough one. Bob does not respond to the usual carrots or sticks. I have known him for a long time"

"Any ideas?"

"Have you tried appealing to his geek pride? He can't be bought but he does get territorial about his stuff."

"That's interesting. Can I threaten to replace him?"

"That won't work. Think about it"

"How about if I bring in someone to help him?"

"Now you are thinking. You need a real person. Have Alice set up some temp agency interviews for you. Maybe if Bob sees you are interviewing some programmers, he will get the hint"

"Okay, thanks"

That was a strategy they did not teach in B school. It could work. Tony went to Alice's desk.

"Hi Alice, can you set me up with a temp agency? I want to interview programmers"

"You have a budget?" Alice guarded the department budget like a grizzly with her cubs.

"I don't. Guido said I should interview some temps to help Bob". He didn't tell her he probably would not actually hire anyone. He wasn't sure how close she and Bob really were and didn't want his planned ruse to get back to him. Besides, if the ruse didn't work, he may really need to hire someone.

"It will have to come out of Guido's budget, I will run it by him"

"Thanks Alice, I appreciate it".

The next day Tony was sitting in his cube discussing the project with Bob.

"Bob you need to pick up the pace, we talked about this"

"It will be done when it is done, you can't rush these things"

"We have deadlines. We promised the customer"

"You promised the customer. You want it right don't you? We always seem to have time to do stuff over but not to do it right from the get go" Bob's response was another one of those tired platitudes Tony was sick of hearing.

Alice walked by and dumped a stack of folders on Tony's desk. Her timing was impeccable. It could not have been better if they had planned it.

"Here's those resumes you wanted from the temp agency"

"How did you get them so fast?"

"I'm Alice. We throw them a lot of business with and they respond pretty quickly to requests. They couriered them right over"

"Thanks Alice"

Bob stared at the pile on the desk "Are we hiring temp sales guys?"

"Nope, these are programmers. Guido gave me budget to get you some help, so we can finish on time. It looks like you might be over committed on this and we don't want to fail."

"But it will take me more time to bring a new guy up to speed than we will gain. Most of this is in my head...." Bob started to protest.

"There are some clever guys here, I am sure we can make it work. Look here is a guy whose last job was at IBM in word processing. He probably has the formatting codes in his head. And hey- this guy is a masters in math from MIT. That's just the first two I picked up. I am sure we will find you suitable help"

"I don't need help" Bob was in full defensive mode.

"I think that you do"

Bob half walked, and half stomped away. Tony hit a nerve. "I hope this works" Tony thought. He did run the risk of Bob getting mad and quitting outright. He thought the odds of that were low given how long Bob worked for the company. Tony set to putting together numbers for a proposal he and Guido were making to an insurance company next week and did not see Bob all afternoon. He hoped that that was a good sign. It could mean he got mad and left the building. Before he knew it, it was five thirty. Tony had to leave at a reasonable time this day. He was taking Madison out to dinner to make up for all the late nights. On his way out, he noticed Bob was still in his cube. He knew before he got near because of the smell of Doritos that hung in the air. There were several pieces of paper taped up all over the cube walls and Bob was typing away like a mad man at his terminal. Tony also noticed several empty coke cans and Doritos bags on the floor. It was a mess in there, but it looks like work was being done.

Tony got home in time for dinner. That had become an unusual thing these days and he knew that it made Madison very happy. The plan was to go out to dinner at the new fish place in town. Tony had been wanting to try it for quite some time now. Bob told him that it had the best Calamari. Madison had other ideas. It was her day off from the bank and she spent the day preparing some favorite dishes, including sautéed calamari. She even drove out to the shore to buy fresh squid. As soon as he walked in the door the smells of dinner hit him in the face. It was a much more pleasant smell than a cube full of Doritos. Tony was never so happy to have been reliable as he was at that moment.

"This place smells fantastic!"

"I am glad you like it. I have been slaving all day. I wanted dinner to be special."

Tony was about to ask why then he remembered "Darn, this is the anniversary of our first date". He wished that he had gotten a card or something. They made a bigger deal out of this than their wedding anniversary.

"I'm sorry, I didn't get you a card or anything"

"That's okay- you've been busy. Did your day go well?" Madison was pretty understanding.

"I think I figured out how to get Bob off the dime on that project. All I had to do was get him help"

"He's working with someone else on it?"

"Not exactly. When it looked like I was getting someone else in he shifted into high gear. Turns out he is pretty territorial."

"That was a good idea. I am proud of you"

"It wasn't entirely my idea" He told about Guido and their discussion.

"Yeah but you did it"

"Thanks, let's not talk about work any more. Remember that place?" Tony changed topics. He knew he manipulated Bob an was surprised that he didn't feel bad about it. He didn't want to deal with that just now.

"What place?"

"The place in Maine we went to on our first date."

"The clam shack? I remember that. We had to fish change out of the car seats to pay the bill because you didn't bring enough money"

"Yup, that place."

On their first date Tony and Madison drove up Route One and stopped at a clam shack in Kittery. They were both still in school and didn't have a lot of money. The clam shack bill was a little more than Tony had on him. They were able to fish enough money out of the car seats and the change in the ashtray to pay the bill. That left no toll money, so they drove back home on back roads and not on the Maine turnpike.

"They are tearing it down to make way for another outlet mall.   This weekend let's go there one more time"

"Let's do that" Madison served the dinner. Tony was a little bit surprised at how good it was. She was not generally a gourmet cook by any means.

"This is really good. I am not just being nice. This is excellent"

"I am glad you like it. Your mother gave me the recipes."

"When did she do that?"

"I visited with her yesterday. Didn't I tell you? We had a very nice time" This shocked Tony more than the food. His mother was still not warmed up the fact that he married Madison. He started to wonder if maybe she was dying.

"She was nice to you?"

"Yes, very nice. We had a great talk and she gave me some recipes"

"Is she dying?"

"That's awful! Whey would you say that?"

"It's just unlike her. She wouldn't share recipes even with her own sister. She guards them like the nuclear launch codes"

"Maybe she just likes me"

"You know her, it's not you, it's any woman, she's an Italian mother no woman is good enough for her boy. I think she's dying"

"You're nuts"

"I'll call her later"

Tony and Madison ate the rest of their dinner. There was even cannollis for dessert. Tony was very happy. He offered to clean up and Madison took him up on the offer. That was new, he didn't often clean up after dinner.

"Hey- why don't you call your mother?"

"It's late"

"It's only seven thirty- she's still up"

Tony dialed the number. A little old lady voice appeared on the other end.

"Hi Ma"

"Who's this?"

"It's Tony Ma"

"Tony? What are you calling so late? Are you okay? Is someone dying? Is it your Aunt Therese?"

"No one's dying Ma"

"What?"

"No one's dying Ma" louder

"Then why are you calling"

"To thank you for the recipes you gave Madison"

"You're calling because you're glad again? What does that mean?"

"No Ma I am calling to thank you for helping Madison" Tony was talking loud enough now that he was sure his mother could hear him without the phone.

"Oh, Madison sure sure. Did everything come out good?"

"Very good Ma"

"She didn't over cook the squid?"

"No Ma- all good"

"You don't need me no more. I am just an old lady. Visit my grave when I die." Tony could sense some amount of jealousy there. He looked over to Madison and mouthed "I am sorry" then told his mother "The pasta was little over done" then shook his head no to Madison.

"She'll learn. I have a lot to teach her" his mother said "I have to go my show is on"

"Bye Ma"

"Bye Antonio"

Tony hung up the phone. "That went well"

"You told her I wrecked the pasta?"

"I had to throw her a bone. She was about to spin up into full martyr mode"

"Why can't you deal with her truthfully? Why do you have to lie to her like that?"

"She's Maria the martyr. Sometimes you just have to play the game her way"

"That's stupid"

"You're not Italian."

"You manipulated Bob, you manipulated your Mother. What are you doing to me?"

Tony smiled and said "You know me too well. I am an open book for you"

CHAPTER 17

A STORM IS COMING

The weather lady stood in front of her big weather map. She was very excited it was like weather lady Christmas. More excited that Tony had ever seen. She waved with both arms and pointed at the map. Tropical storm Walter was now category three hurricane Walter and coming our way. It was following the east coast and would cross over land in Connecticut. The excited weather lady said that winds will be over eighty miles an hour and there will be driving rain when it got to Tony's place sometime in the next few hours. There wasn't much Tony could do about it. These things targeted trailer parks but he was't moving. He moved all his outdoor stuff inside except for his folding chair. He would move that in later. He noticed Lorraine had moved all her stuff inside. The garden gnome across the way looked as smug as ever.

Tony grabbed a beer and sat out on his folding chair. He put a CD of BB King in his little CD player. The sky was the color of an old nickel that had been left out in the yard. The wind was starting to pick up. To him it felt to be about thirty or so miles per hour already. The trees he could see were oscillating back and forth. He eyed the old pine across the way. It was within striking distance of his place. He hoped it would not fall on him. "I am sure it has seen its share of hurricanes and northeasters" he said to himself. He felt the first drops of rain rolling down his brow and took a long swig on his beer.

"You playing that girly bar music again?" Lorraine was at her window.

"BB King"

"Girly bar music"

"As you wish"

"Haven't you watched the weather? There's a hurricane. Get in out of the rain!!"

"I have watched the weather Lorraine. That's why I am out here. I'm waiting for the rain"

"Well. it's here. Get inside you idiot". She must have put her insult thesaurus away.

"Why don't you come out here?"

""Cause I am not crazy"

"Not that kind of crazy anyway" Tony thought to himself.

"Suit yourself" he said out loud.

The rain still was starting to come down harder and the wind picked up a lot just in the time they were talking. Tony finished his beer and glared over at the garden gnome.

"Enjoy the storm you smug little piece of yard art" The garden gnome just stared back with that same annoying close mouth smile and slightly tilted head.

Tony folded up his lawn chair and went inside. He opened another beer and flipped on the TV. The weather lady was still on the TV. They went to a remote reporter standing on the sea wall in Gloucester. Waves were splashing up around him and the wind was driving rain in his face. The cameraman kept needing to wipe the lens. The reporter looks like he was just short of getting blown away. The wind was worst at the ocean. The reporter was warning people to stay away from the shore. "So why are you there?" Tony thought to himself. It didn't make sense to him to have a guy there, all they had to do was sit in the nice, dry, warm studio and say it was bad. Why risk the crew and the reporter? Then he remembered, spectacle, circuses. It sold TV time. Even if they would not admit it to themselves people got a thrill out of seeing someone in danger. It was the twenty first century version of the coliseum games. Far less blood was shed though. Also, fewer wild beasts. We are a little more civilized, allegedly. They then switched to a reporter at the emergency management center. The state had a center somewhere underground in Framingham or somewhere like that. Tony never bothered to learn where exactly. He didn't really need to know. It was an impressive set up. There were rows and rows of people with headphones sitting at computers and big video displays at the front showing weather, traffic and the locations of problems. All aimed to show the people that the state was in control. For all anyone knew those rows and rows of people were playing World of Warcraft on those computers. Don't fret, citizen. Whenever there was a big weather event the governor and the head of the state police would go there to "manage the emergency". They must stock Mr. Rogers style sweaters there because the governor always managed to have one on for the camera. Tony figured he thought it was more comforting to the general populace if the governor looked relaxed. It was a nice sweater all told. Of course, he could look relaxed a big old pine tree wasn't about to fall on his house. He was twenty feet underground. Tony, on the other hand, lived in a glorified storage container set up on cinderblocks surrounded by other tin cans. And, of course there was that big pine tree. Hurricanes and tornadoes target parks like his all the time. They hate trailer parks. Trailer parks did something bad to their mothers. The governor came on the TV and gave the usual "stay indoors, keep the streets open for emergency vehicles, power company has extra crews, blah blah blah blah. After about five minutes all Tony heard was noise.

"Holy cow that wind is getting strong" Tony said out loud to no one. Not that someone there would have heard him, the wind was loud. It was whistling through the gaps around his door. His kitchen window was rattling with every gust. Tony could hear the banging of loose siding on his trailer and the occasional tree limb snapping. The rain was executing drum rolls on his metal roof. He even thought he felt the trailer shaking a little. Suddenly there was a loud thud and the ground shook a little. "Earthquake?" was the first thing Tony thought. It didn't last as long as the only other earthquake Tony had ever been in. That earthquake happened when he was in San Francisco back in eighty-nine. It lasted around fifteen seconds. This one was just a single big thud. Strange, he thought, earthquakes are usually a little longer than one thud. There was a banging on his door. It was Lorraine.

"Are you okay in there?"

"Yes, why wouldn't I be? What are you doing out in this weather?" he opened the door and let her in.

"That big pine came down, didn't you hear it?"

"I didn't hear anything." then he realized what that big thud was, it was no earthquake it was an about one-hundred-year-old white pine falling. It didn't hit his trailer. Score one for Tony.

"I thought it hit your trailer"

"I guess it didn't" Tony replied.

"It came pretty darn close"

Tony put on his shoes and his rain coat and went outside. Sure, enough the tree fell right between his place and the next neighbor, someone was looking out for him. It did no damage. Not even to the smug garden gnome across the way. He could even get his car out if he needed to go somewhere. Nothing he could, or needed to, do about it now. He went back inside.

"Do you want a beer Lorraine?"

"Sure, you got one?"

" What do you think, why would I offer.... never mind?"

Tony went to the fridge and brought Lorraine a beer. She cleared some magazines off of his couch and sat down. She looked for a coaster and settled on a magazine. Tony was surprised. He found that table on the side of the road on trash day. No number of can ring stains was going to make it any worse.

"So, did you call that woman?" Lorraine was nosey.

"None of your business, but yes I did"

"How did it go? Are you going to see her again?"

"Maybe".

"You have to see her again, don't be a wuss"

"Maybe"

"Hey, look at this fool". The TV caught Lorraine's attention it had switched back to the guy at the sea wall. "He's going to get washed out to sea. You don't want that. My friend got washed out to sea and they never found him. They said it was the rip tide, but I know it was aliens. Aliens have flying saucers that hide under the water. He had one of those implants the aliens put in you. I saw it on X-Files"

"You know that stuff isn't real, Right?"

"Oh, it's real alright. You've been brainwashed"

Tony knew not to argue. He and Lorraine sat in silence for a while and finished their beers. He was about to get up an get them another one.

"I have to go back home; the dog will be worried"

"Do you want to use my blue umbrella?"

"No. I'll be fine. You go see that woman. Not now, you'd be an idiot, but when the storm is over"

Lorraine opened the door to leave. The wind almost pulled her away. Tony grabbed the door and watched as Lorraine scooted across the way to her trailer.

The storm went on for a few more hours. The power went out in various part of the state, according to the TV, Tony did not lose his power. Score another one for Tony. He was starting to feel lucky. First the tree misses him then he doesn't lose power. Maybe he will give Jessica a call and see how she is doing.

Jessica answered her phone. "Tony, are you okay?"

"I am better than okay. A tree missed my trailer, I still have power and Lorraine didn't drink all of my beer. How are you?"

"I've been better. We don't have power and they are saying it will be at least a day. I just went shopping and I have a bunch of groceries going bad. The grandkids are a little house nuts. No TV to watch."

"Bring your stuff over here. My fridge is pretty empty, and the kids can watch my TV. I don't have cable though."

"Can they bring their Nintendo?"

"What's a Nintendo?"

"You're serious? It's a video game. You hook it up to the TV and play"

"Sure- bring it all."

"Thanks, I appreciate this."

"You're welcome"

Tony hung up the phone and wondered whether he had done the right thing. "I better clean this place up!". He grabbed a trash bag and started just dumping stuff into it. He did not realize how many empty beer cans were laying around until he had to pick them all up. There was a knock at the door. It was Jessica. He let her in along with two little humans. There was a girl with curly black hair and a boy, slightly taller, with very short hair that in Tony's day would have been called a "whiffle".

"Hi Tony, this is Jennifer and Michael. Kids say hello to Mr. Sincero"

The two kids looked at their feet and wiggled back and forth for about ten seconds.

"Kids"

"Hello Mr SIncero" in unison.

"Hi kids, you may call me Tony."

"Tony, Tony eats baloney" Michael responded. Jessica gave him the grandmother look and he stopped.

"Can the kids hook up their game to your TV?"

"Sure, why don't you give it to me and I will take care of it". Tony took the video game and hooked it up to the TV. The kids started playing.

"Do you want a beer?" Tony offered Jessica

"The kids......"

"Yes, of course, I'm an idiot- how about coffee?"

"Coffee would be good. Thanks".

"Decaf or regular?"

"Decaf if you have it"

"You got it"

Tony went into the kitchen and set up the coffee maker. It still had coffee in it from earlier, so he had to wash it out. If it was just for him, he would not bother being so careful He would just give it a quick rinse. Because it was for Jessica, he decided he would go all out to make the best impression. He did not think it was good form to make her sick so soon after the way he disappointed her after the concert.

"That's a big tree that came down. There were trees like that down all over town. I had to make several detours to get here" Jessica's apartment was not very far away from Tony's place. She lived over by the library.

"I was lucky" Tony replied as he filled the coffee filter with the fresh grounds. "That thing could have crushed me and my trailer"

"I am glad you are alright. Thanks again for letting me put stuff in your fridge and for letting the kids play their game on your TV. The power guys say we should be back on tomorrow. I just spent a whole paycheck on food and would hate for it to spoil"

Tony added the water to the coffee maker and turned it on, Happy gurgling again. "I don't mind at all, as you can see, I don't have much in my fridge"

"I guess not. I saw beer, sandwich meat, moldy cheese and little else"

"I haven't been shopping in a while"

"Nana can we have a snack?" Jennifer yelled out from over by the TV.

"You can have a pudding. Come and take one for your brother too"

"Nana, they call you nana?" Tony smiled at the name.

"Yes, it's a family thing. I called my grand mother Nana"

"That's cool, are your folk's old country?"

"My family lived in this town for three generations on my father's side. My mother came here with her family from Puerto Rico during the war. They met working at the GE plant in Lowell"

"Do you speak Spanish?"

"My father would not let our mother teach us Spanish growing up"

"Bummer. My parents are both from the old country. They did not want me speaking Italian. I was born here, and they wanted me to blend in. I learned a little around the house because that's all they spoke to each other"

"Are they still around?"

"My mother is, she's too mean to die. My father passed on a few years ago"

"Sorry to hear about your father"

"Me too. My mother is in a home not far from here. I visit her now and then. She does not want to speak to me. I am a great disappointment."

"How so?"

"First by marrying someone who was not from her village and not even Italian then making it worse by being divorced. She disowned me"

"She must be up there in years; can't you get her to reconcile?"

"She is one hundred and six. Okay. I lied. She's eighty-five and her name is Maria"

"Does she see your daughter?"

"No. My daughter lives in Ohio and doesn't get out here much. Her name is also Maria"

"You named her after your mother?"

"It's old world tradition. It didn't make her happy though"

"That's so sad."

'What about you? Where is your daughter? You don't have to answer if you don't want to talk about it. I understand"

"No, no that's okay. I have come to terms with it all. My daughter is called Karen. She is a sweet girl but became addicted to pain killers after a car accident a few years ago. She was a nurse, so she had access to pills until she got caught. Her husband couldn't handle it and walked out on her and the kids. I was able to get custody of the kids, he vanished. It took six months of fighting with the state, but we finally got her into a rehab program. She lives out in Worcester at a halfway house now. We can visit her some weekends. She his not ready to come home yet. I live in a one-bedroom apartment. I don't know what we will do when she gets out. She lost her nursing license and probably cannot get it back. Who would hire her anyway?. I guess we will cross that bridge when we get there" Tony could see a little tear in her eye and sense the pain in her voice. "TMI, let's talk about something else" she said. "I don't want to burden you with my problem. What did you think of the concert?"

"It was great, Francey just keeps getting better and better. Did you enjoy him?"

"Yes, I did"

Jennifer cam running over "Michael won't let me play"

"Michael, you let your sister play too"

"But she doesn't know how, and it ruins the game"

"Let her play anyway!"

"Hey Michael" Tony knew little bit about seven-year-old boys "Why don't you let your sister play the game and I will let you play with my own special truck" Tony still kept a toy dump truck that he had since he was a kid. He went out to the back and got it out.

"This is cool! It's made out if real metal! Where did you get this?" Michael's eyes were huge as he looked at the dome truck.

"I've had it since I was about your age. You can play with it while you are here"

"Wow, thanks Mr Tony". Tony decided "Mr. Tony" was an okay name.

"Have fun"

"Yeah thanks! bucka bucker bucka" Michael made truck noises and rolled the truck around the floor.

"You're not bad with kids" Jessica sounded a little surprised.

"I'm a kid whisperer" Tony chuckled.

Tony and Jessica talked for the next three or four hours. They were three or four of the better hours Tony remembers ever having.

Jessica said "I am going to run home with the kids and get them in bed. Thanks for the use of the fridge."

"Take this flashlight just in case"

"Thanks, see you later"

Jessica and Tony stood staring at each other for what seemed like an hour but was probably fifteen seconds. After the other night they were not sure what to do. Tony leaned in and kissed Jessica on the mouth. rather than pulling back Jessica kissed back.

"See you tomorrow"

Jessica left with the two kids. The kids turned and waved, and both yelled "Thank you Mr. Tony" in unison. Tony waved back and said, "Be good for your Nana kids".

Chapter 18

Another Presentation

Tony's ruse with the contract shop worked. The three weeks were just about up. Bob had been working harder, and eating more Doritos, than Tony had ever seen in the short time that he knew him. He was even skipping his D&D nights.

"How are you doing Bob?"

"It's coming together. I just need to get this last function debugged"

"Great when can we demo it to Guido and Mike?"

"Right after lunch, I will set it up"

"Thanks"

Everyone but Bob went to the Knickerbocker for lunch. Bob stayed back and set up the demo. He ended up having extra time to set up. Mike was in a good mood and bought an extra round for everyone in the department. By the time they got back to work it was mid afternoon and they were all in a good mood. Tony was surprised that Bob wasn't envious of everyone. Extra drinks at lunch was one of his favorite things.

"Sorry you missed the long lunch Bob, I know it's one of your favorite things" Tony was not being sarcastic. He was actually sorry.

"I'll make up for it later. I wanted to set this up. It's all good to go in the conference room"

"I'll grab Guido and Mike and meet you there"

Bob went to the conference room to wait. About ten minutes later Guido, Mike and Tony rolled in. Bob noticed Tony was a little redder faced than the other two. All three of them were showing the affects of a long lunch.

"Okay Bobby what do you have for us" This is the first time Mike ever called him Bobby.

They gathered around the the terminal. Bob ran through all the features that had asked him to create and then a couple he created on his own.

"They didn't ask for this, but it was easy to do. I added a time stamp feature to show when and by whom a document was translated"

"Why did you do that if no one asked for it?"

"I was having trouble tracking my sample documents and thought if I was having trouble with a few docs they may have trouble with larger numbers of them."

"Does it still run in the memory allocated?"

"Yes, it does. I also made some of the other code more efficient"

"That's great Bobby. Thanks" Mike was happy "When can you guys present this to the bank people?"

"We have a meeting day after tomorrow"- Tony had it set up already.

Two days later Tony, Mike, Guido and Bob were gathered in that same conference room with the gaggle of bankers and Sandy. Alice brought in some coffee and donuts. The alpha banker reached over and grabbed a jelly donut. Leaning back in his seat he said

"You guys are done when you said you would be. That's a good sign. As long as it works. How are we going to know it works?"

"We have some sample docs we will translate for you." Bob replied.

"How do I know the translation from you to IBM worked? I don't see an IBM here"

"I have the codes- I can show you the differences"

"Not good enough"

Sandy realized that it may be spiraling out of control. Alpha banker was not very technical. He would need to see it on paper. She liked Tony and wanted to go with this product. She also thought that it was the best solution.

"I can bring the documents back to the bank and check them on the loaner" Sandy said. Now Tony and Guido knew that IBM had given the bank a demo system. Not a good sign.

Mike knew it too. "Gentlemen let me confer with my colleagues` for a minute outside. Make yourself comfortable. Should I have Alice bring more coffee?"

The gaggle of bankers all nodded "no" in unison like some kind of automated Christmas display.

"Bob, do we still have that small R2 prototype? Can your stuff run on that?" Tony was the first to speak

"Yes, we do, why?"

"I was thinking we could have Bob set that system up at the bank and train Sandy to use it. I doubt IBM has a guy on site there every day. We could have Bob there any time they wanted"

Mike liked that idea. "Let's do that"

"I am not a field service guy" Bob objected.

"This is not a field service job Bob, we are making you an applications engineer" Guido said, imagining that 'applications engineer' sounded better to Bob.

"That sounds okay then" it did sound better to Bob.

They rejoined the meeting and proposed this plan to the gaggle of bankers. The alpha banker was pretty happy with the idea, so the rest of the gaggle went right along with it.

Sandy asked "Will Tony be on site as well"

Before Tony could answer for himself Mike said, "If you need him, of course he will".

Mike brought Tony, Guido and Bob down to the executive dining room. They sat at one of the round tables near to the windows. Mike held up four fingers. A waiter came over with four glasses of Bourbon. Straight up. Mike was in charge and when he was buying you drank what he drank. No questions asked.

"That went well today, here's to you guys" Mike held up his glass. "We are on the five-yard line and it's third down. Let's not screw this up, Bob will bring that R2 system over there tomorrow and set it up for Sandy. Show her how to work with the new programs Bob"

"Okay. I still have a lot of wiring closet stuff and I have to set up the new guy here. I have been ignoring that work to do this for the last month"

"You're done with that work Bob, I am hiring your replacement. I want you on customers"

"But Mike......" Bob started to object.

"It's done" Mike gets what Mike wants.

Mike waved to the waiter and got another round brought over and a third. Tony did not object. He was proud of their work.

"Tony, you did a bang-up job on this. I am putting you in charge of the North East territory."

"But Mike, that's Porter's job" Guido said with just a hint of joy.

"Porter is moving to the west coast. His wife has family out there and he asked to be transferred. The West Coast guy quit to work for some start up. No loyalty, he'll never work for me again"

Guido slapped Tony on the back and said "You lucky SOB, you haven't been here a year and we are peers! Congratulations"

"No one has ever advanced this quickly. I have a lot of confidence in you, don't let me down. "Mike added.

Tony went home that night happy as anything and a little tipsy. It was the couch again for him.

CHAPTER 19

AFTER THE STORM

Ringinginginging Ringinginginging. The sound of a chain saw right outside his window woke a startled Tony. He sat straight up in bed and threw his hands over his ears. This trailer was pretty good at keeping the rain out, but sound was a whole other thing. At first, he wasn't sure what was going on. "Oh yeah, the tree", he remembered. The park maintenance guys were out there cutting up that big pine. It was eleven o'clock already. Jessica and the kids didn't leave until late last night. He was shocked that he slept so late just the same. Part of what he paid to live in his trailer went to maintenance things like this. Tony felt good to be getting something for his money. He put on some pants, a shirt and the coffee maker and went outside.

They were cutting away the part of the tree that blocked the road. When the chain saws stopped Tony yelled over "You guys want a cup of coffee".

"No thanks, we are almost done here, and we have two more to do as quickly as we can" The man that answered was half again Tony's size and holding a chain saw. None the less Tony replied

"Are you going to take away the whole tree?"

"Not planning on it, we are just clearing the road, the rest stays"

"You're not taking the rest of it?"

"We are leaving it where it lays"

"It is in the way. My neighbor can just barely get out of his door"

"Talk to my boss"

Tony went inside to have coffee. He would give the park office a call. It isn't really the worker's fault he was just doing what he was told, he supposed. He didn't know the neighbor on that side very well. Not like he knew Lorraine. His door and Lorraine's door faced each other. The other neighbor faced the back of his trailer, so Tony did not have the occasion to talk with him often. All Tony knew about was he was elderly and drove a Buick that was even older than his.

After he had his coffee Tony gave the management office a call.

"Hi, this is Antonio Sincero on Madison. A tree came down next to my trailer...."

"We sent guys out there to clear it!" The voice on the other end interrupted.

"Yes, and they cleared the roadway but left most of the tree in between me and my neighbor"

"Look, it's a busy time we have a lot of clean up...."

"Yes, yes I know that I just want to know if it will ever be cleaned up" It was Tony's turn to interrupt.

"We will get to it in a few weeks"

"That's all I ask, thanks" Tony hung up.

Tony poured his second cup of coffee and sat down to watch the television. The news people were busy showing footage of the storm damage and being amazed at the damage estimates. After about fifteen minutes of this Tony had enough and shut the TV off. "These people aren't helping anyone" he thought. He was just about to switch from coffee to beer when the phone rang. It was Jessica.

"Hello"

"Hi, It's Jessica"

"HI Jessica, how are you? How are the kids?"

"We are all fine. Are you busy today?"

"I'm not busy any days, what's up" That was mostly true. Except for pretending to job hunt and the occasional favor for Lorraine his days were pretty free.

"One of the older women in my church had some damage from the storm and some us are going there to help repair her house. She is on a fixed income and can't afford much. Are you any good with carpentry?"

"My father was a handyman of sorts. He didn't have much money so did a lot of work himself and did a lot of work for the neighbors. He taught me a thing or two"

"That's great, I will come by and get you."

The house they were fixing belonged to a very interesting widowed woman named Anne. The house she lived in was up on a hill. It was built in the early twentieth century. A tree and fallen in the storm and damaged part of the wrap around porch. When they got there two men had already cut the tree away and removed it. They were staring at the damage to the porch roof. Tony stood staring at the roof along side of them.

"Bill, Charlie, this is my friend Tony. He came along to help" Jessica introduced Tony. "He knows some about carpentry"

"Good, cause we don't know much" Bill was smiling.

"The first thing we need to do is take a lot of photos for the insurance people then we should water proof this as much as possible. The right thing to do will be to get insurance to send an adjuster and then get the proper permits before we do any fixing"

"That's all well and good but Anne doesn't have insurance to cover this" Charlie said.

"The church has an emergency fund and we can buy some materials, but we need labor"

"Fair enough, let's get some beers and get to work" Tony was ready.

"No beers, we are both in recovery, but we can get to work"

"No beers it is, let's start by clearing out the broken bits and see what we need"

It had been a long long time since Tony worked as physically hard as this. Bill and Charlie were about the same age as he and they were a couple of the hardest workers Tony had known. They got a lot of work done and had a lot more to go but they were losing daylight.

"I think we can finish this tomorrow or maybe the next day if you two are available" Hard work and not drinking all day felt pretty good to Tony. He was surprised.

"What time can you be here?" Charlie asked.

"As early as you fellows can"

"Eight o'clock then?"

"See you then"

Tony and Jessica left in Jessica's car. They waved over to Bill and Charlie as they pulled out of the driveway. By now it was getting dark, so they may not have even seen them.

"That was actually quite fun. I like those guys" Tony said.

"They are hard workers. It seems they liked you as well. I thought you were a sales guy; how did you learn to do this kind of work?" Jessica replied.

"When I was growing up my dad did any kind of extra work, he could to make ends meet. I went on a lot of the side jobs with him and helped. He was always exhausted, and it beat him up physically. Often, he worked his full-time job and nights an weekends to get us by. He pushed me to do better, he didn't want that life for me. He made sure I could go to college. He wanted me to be a big shot and I didn't want to let him down." Tony replied with maybe more than Jessica asked.

"You worked hard today." Jessica responded.

"It felt good. Do you want to get something to eat?" Tony asked.

"I need to get the kids"

"What do they like? Let's bring them along "

"Are you sure?"

"I'm Mr. Tony" They both laughed.

CHAPTER 20

TONY GETS PROMOTED

Tony could smell coffee. He rolled over and fell on to the floor. He forgot he was on the couch. He tried to get up and realized he was tangled up in the blankets. He looks like a fish caught in a net trying to get out. Madison must have covered him up in the night. She also must have taken his shoes off. He was still dressed in his work clothes.

"Do you want coffee?"

He fought to get his arms untangled so he could rub the sleep from his eyes. "Ummm... sure". Maybe coffee would would get the cotton out of his mouth, He also had a bit of a headache.

"Did I sleep on the couch last night?"

"What do you think? You don't remember?"

"I'm a little fuzzy. Did I tell you I got a promotion?"

"Bob drove you home. He said you and your boss were celebration something to do with a big deal"

"Bob drove me home? Why did he do that?"

"He said you were on no shape and he knew what no shape looked like. He was barely in shape to drive. I am surprised the two of you didn't end up in jail" Madison did not sound pleased.

"I guess I need to thank him when I get in"

"He's in the spare room you can thank him when he gets up"

"Bob gets the spare room and I get the couch?"

"Right now, I am liking Bob a little better than I am liking you"

"Did I tell you I got promoted?"

"You mentioned it. Are we moving?"

"Nope, I am in charge of the North East region" Tony got a sudden wave of nausea and ran to the bathroom.

"Are you okay in there?"

"I will be, sorry"

Bob came out of the spare room looking pretty bright eyed.

"How come you didn't get as drunk as your buddy in there?" Madison asked.

"I have known Guido and Mike for a long time. I know better than to try to go drink for drink with them."

"I guess my husband doesn't"

"I am going to shower and clean up" Tony yelled from the bathroom.

"Please do that" Madison replied.

"Bob, coffee?"

"Please I would love some coffee"

Bob sat down at kitchen table and Madison poured him some coffee.

"Cream and sugar?"

"Yes, thanks"

"You guys drink an awful lot at that place, should I be worried?"

"Don't worry Madison, it's no big deal. Mike likes to celebrate big contracts with his guys and Tony has gotten a couple of huge ones lately. That's why they promoted him. He's a good salesman"

"I'm getting worried"

"No problem"

"So, what is this promotion he was talking about? "

"I should let him tell you. Hey, is that bacon I smell?"

"Could be, what do you know about this promotion. It seems unusual that he would be promoted so soon"

"This guy Porter, who most folks including Mike cannot stand, transferred to the west coast. His job opened, and Mike decided that Tony could do it. It's no big deal to Mike. If Tony doesn't do well, he will transfer him to the midwest somewhere. He does this all the time with guys he thinks have potential"

"Bacon, I smell bacon" Tony was out of the shower and dressed.

"Bob told me about your promotion"

"He did, did he?"

"Yes, it sounds pretty good. I know you can handle it. You're very smart"

"I don't feel real smart right now. Bob- can you give us privacy for a minute?"

"Yup" Bob took his eggs and bacon and went to the other room.

"I want to apologize for last night. It won't happen again. I promise"

"It's been happening a lot. Don't promise what you can't deliver. I am not one of your sales prospects"

"I can deliver, it's just that office politics requires a certain amount of socializing...."

"Maybe you could socialize a little smarter. You have responsibilities at home"

"I know, I know"

"Tony- I am expecting"

"Expecting? Expecting what?" Tony was still foggy.

"A baby you moron"

This wasn't in the plan, but Tony was excited. More excited than he had thought he would be. He wrapped his arms around Madison and held her tightly. He didn't let go for a couple of minutes.

CHAPTER 21

MCDONALDS

Tony and Jessica went and picked up the kids. They decided to take them to the big McDonalds with the playroom. Not exactly haute cuisine but they figured the kids could play in the big ball pit and Jessica and Tony could talk more. The kids were very excited. It was a treat for them to go to McDonalds and they liked Tony. Tony bought them both a burger and fries in one of those little boxes that came with a toy, Jessica insisted they drink water so no soda for them. When they finished their food, they asked to play in the ball pit.

"Go ahead but make sure I can see you at all times" Jessica was a strict Nana.

"They are great kids"

"They're not bad. They don't know you really well, so they are on their best behavior"

"How long have you known Anne?"

"Only about fifteen years. That house has been in her family for two or three generations."

"She seems like a nice woman"

"She's yankee stock. She raised three strong headed boys after her husband passed. They are rugged men but will cower when she speaks for sure" Jessica laughed.

"I won't mess with her then. Bill and Charlie, you know them long?"

"Only a few years. They are both recovering alcoholics trying to get their stuff together. Nice enough guys. I didn't know them in the old days. There are stories"

"Interesting stories?"

"I am told one-time Bill snuck out the back of a bar in Lowell during a fight and could not find his car. The police had come to break up the fight and left their cars idling outside of the bar. Bill decided that it was a good idea to drive one of the police cars home. The neighbors called the cops the next morning to ask why a police car had been in their neighborhood all night with the motor running."

"What happened to Bill?"

"They couldn't prove it was him, he got away with it"

"That's kind of funny. I have never done anything that bad." Tony was lying. One time before he left his last sales job, he had so much to drink with a customer that they both ended up spending the night as guests of the town. His boss was okay with it, but the customer ended up getting fired. In the long run it cost Tony a contact and probably that client. It wasn't the only time he'd been an idiot. He decided not to tell Jessica about it.

"Both guys are reformed now and doing pretty well. They don't touch a drop"

"I still do but I can handle it" Tony's voice had a hint of question in it.

"Are you sure?" That's as far as Jessica was willing to pursue this line of discussion. The kids came over.

"Nana- can we have some quarters for the claw machine?" The game room had one of those claw machines that gives you a chance to get a cheap toy.

"Those things never work"

"Aww, c'mon Nana!!"

"If it is okay with your Nana, I have three quarters and we will each take one turn" Tony looked over at Jessica hoping he hadn't spoken out of turn.

"Okay you three- have fun"

Michael went first, He had an eye on a stuffed cat that looked pretty loose on the top of the pile. He put his quarter in the machine and deftly maneuvered the claw over the stuffed cat. When he was happy with the location, he pressed the drop button. The claw came down right on top of the stuffed cat and grabbed it by the head but when it lifted back up the claws didn't grab. Michael huffed and stepped back from the machine. "Stupid machine"

Next it was Jennifer's turn. Tony found a step stool for her to stand on she gave it a try. She randomly pushed the buttons and the claw dropped down on a plastic bracelet. The bracelet hung precariously off of one of the claw arms and wiggled back and forth like a pendulum as the claw traversed over to the drop zone. It was looking like she was going to be successful! Just before it was over the drop zone the bracelet wiggled off and fell back on the pile of toys. Jennifer said, "That's not fair!" and banged her hand on the machine.

"Mr. Tony, it's all up to you, you're our last hope!" Jessica pleaded. Tony knew that the odds of getting anything were slim to none. He had read how the machines were rigged to only grip tightly every once in a while.

"Well kids. I will try. These things are harder than it looks" They were too little for him to explain that the whole thing was rigged. Tony put in his quarter and went to work. There was a stuffed duck that looked pretty promising over to one corner. He manipulated the gantry to be over the duck and pressed the button. The claw came down and grabbed onto that duck tightly. The two kids were on tippy toes at either side of the machine watching intently. As the claw rose with its treasure and started back to the drop point they held their breath and jumped up and down. When it got to the drop point it released its prize into the well. Tony took it out and handed it to the kids. "You'll have to share"" He said.

Michael said, "Let Jennifer have it, she likes ducks". Tony was impressed at his generosity.

"Nana, Nana Mr Tony did it!!" both kids bounded back to Jessica bouncing up and down like Impalas, the animal not the car.

Jessica looked up at Tony and mouthed "Thank you" then said out loud "How did you do that?"

Tony replied, "It's my lucky day" There was no skill or magic just good old-fashioned dumb luck. Jessica saw that Tony liked her grandkids. It was his lucky day.

CHAPTER 22

MADISON LUNCHES WITH HER MOTHER

"Hi Mother, it's Madison"

"Yes, I do know your voice dear"

"Are you free for lunch?"

"Today?"

"Yes today"

"Where?"

"How about that new grille place? At Noon?"

"Yes, that sounds good dear- see you there"

The Grille, as it was called, had only recently opened. The restaurant was divided into two sections. One side had dinner seating and the other was a lounge area with a bar, bumper pool table and juke box. Madison got there a few minutes early and asked for a seat in the back of the dining room. She was pretty sure her mother would like the food there. It was very American. Her mother was not a big fan of Asian fusion food which was one of the other choices around, or actually a fan of any food she considered "too heathen".

Madison's mother showed up promptly at noon and found her in the back of the restaurant.

"Hello dear"

"Hello Mother"

"Shall we order some wine? Red or white? What do you think you will have for lunch? I have heard that they have a grilled salmon that is very good"

"No wine for me mom but you may go right ahead"

"No wine with lunch? Are you feeling okay dear?"

"Yes Mother, I am fine."

"Your father and I are planning a trip to the island next month, why don't you come along?"

"Tony can't take off work."

"Come without him Dear, it will be fun"

"I am working too Mother"

"Are you still working your little bank job? I thought you would be bored of that by now"

"I'm not, plus we need the money right now"

"We can give you money and you have your trust fund"

"We've been over this Mother"

"Don't be silly, come with"

"Mother I have something I need to tell you"

"What is it dear?"

"Mother, I am pregnant"

"Oh my, I was afraid of this. Any chance Tony is not the father?"

"Mother, Tony is the father, he is the only one that could be the father!"

"Oh well, one can hope. I've always liked the Cabot kid at the club."

"Mother!" Madison was whisper yelling.

The waiter came by "Are you ready to order ladies?". The two-woman waved him off and continued their conversation.

"We have a doctor that can take care of this. No one needs to know"

"I will know Mother, Tony will know Mother"

"We so hoped you would be over this Tony fellow before something like this happened. What are we going to do?"

"You are going to mind your business, not say anything bad to to Tony and love this baby"

"Of course, we will love the baby, we just wished it would have had a better pedigree"

"Mother, it's your grandchild, not a dog!"

"I know it's not a dog. Think of your future!! Do you want to be trapped as house wife with no prospects and this fool of a husband?"

"I am not trapped Mother and I love Tony"

"You will be trapped, and you will get over Tony, I guarantee"

The waiter came back to take their orders.

"What can I get you ladies?"

Madison stood up and grabbed her purse. She said, "Nothing for me" and walked out of the restaurant.

Tony was home from work early that night, still pretty excited about the baby.

"Did you see your mother at lunch?"

"Yes"

"Well, did you tell her? What did she say?"

"I don't want to talk about it"

"Why?"

"We had a fight in the restaurant. She was not very supportive."

"She was not excited to be a grandma? "

"Not exactly. She will warm up to it though. I am sure"

"I hope so"

Madison was smart enough to not tell Tony how her parents really felt about him. Tony, on the other hand, didn't need to be told. Madison and he were from different worlds. Madison grew up with money, good schools and relatives with connections. Tony was the son of immigrants. He went to public schools in what was not the most prestigious of towns. He went to a state college before B.U. He didn't have the connections and the upbringing that Madison had. He was a little too rough around the edges for her parents. Her parents were far too polite and polished to ever say anything to him. He could tell by the looks and whispers. One time when they were dating Tony was invited to a family get together. It was formal and required a suit and a tie. Tony only owned one suit and one tie. They were both hand me downs from a cousin who was a couple years older. They did not fit perfectly. Tony looked like a little kid wearing his father's stuff. It also did not help that the jacket and the tie were on the bold side of loud. At the family gathering all of Madison's family was dressed in tailored suits and power ties. Even the littlest kids had expensive suits. Tony could see the looks and sense that even Madison was embarrassed. He swore to himself that he would never let himself be in that position again. He would have the expensive suits and power ties someday.

"Listen. I know your parents do not really care for me. I know they are nice to me because they care for you. That's okay. I can deal with that. I just want to know that they will love this baby and treat him or her like family regardless of how they feel about me"

"They will, I am sure of it. Who cares what they think anyway? I love you and we are together"

Tony was a happy, if scared, guy. He would have suggested a toast, but Madison was not drinking any more. They just sat on the couch together quietly staring at the wall. Tony was remembering his childhood and how hard his father worked and that he hardly saw him. He wanted it to be different with his kid. He wanted to be there. He also wanted his kid to have the kind of opportunities Madison had to go to good schools and want for nothing.

CHAPTER 23

TONY CALLS MARIA

Spending time with Jessica and her grandkids made Tony sad to think about what he was missing. He hadn't tried to call Maria in months. Maria was living in Ohio with her two kids and her husband. Her husband worked for a small machine shop out there and Maria was a secretary. He had never seen it, but he was told they live in a nice little ranch house on a quiet street. He would like to see it some day. Maybe he should try calling. He got out his cell phone and looked up the number. He hoped she was still in the same place. He scrolled on the contact page until he found her. He went to touch the little symbol that would dial her number and his finger froze. It was like there was an invisible force field over the phone. He took a deep breath. Then another one. And another one. He could feel his heart rate slowing down. "Maybe I will have a drink before I call" he thought. "Not a good idea" the imaginary angel on his shoulder responded. "When did the angel on my shoulder start sounding like Jessica?" he asked himself. "Okay so no drink". He pushed the virtual button and held the phone to his ear. There was ringing.

"Hello"

"Hello Maria, it's your Dad"

"What do you want?" he swore he could hear ice in her voice.

"How are you doing? How are my grandkids?"

"Have you been drinking?"

"No" Tony realized it has been a couple of days since he had a drink "not for a few days actually"

"That's good. Are you in a program?"

"Not really"

"Why the big change?"

"I am not sure. I've been busy, I spent some time with a new friend and her grand children today and it reminded me how much I would like to see my own"

"You know the rule Dad"

"Yes, I know". Maria did not want Tony near the kids until he was in a program and sober. He never thought there was an issue. "Can I talk to the kids?"

"Not now, they are outside. Maybe another time"

Maria's husband, Frank, came into the room from the garage where he was fixing the car. He was wearing coveralls and both his hands were greasy.

"Who's that?"

Maria said "excuse me" to her Dad and cupped her hand over the phone "It's my dad"

"What does he want?"

"The same as always, talk to the kids"

"I don't want that lush upsetting our kids....and you"

"He's their grandfather, he deserves to get to know them"

"When I see the one-year coin maybe then"

"It's not just your call you know"

"You know you feel the same as me"

She put the phone back to her ear "Dad I have to go."

"Okay, can we talk later?"

"We'll see". Maria hung up the phone.

Frank was still standing in the kitchen. "Maria, you know how I feel about that guy"

"Frank, he's their grandfather, he's my father"

"He gave that up years ago. He should have thought of that before our wedding. He should have thought of that when you were growing up"

"Maybe he is really trying?"

"I will believe it when I see it" Frank turned back to go to the garage. "What time is dinner? I have a couple more hours work on that Buick". Frank was restoring an old Riviera.

Tony put down the phone and grabbed a beer from the fridge. "That went well" he said but no one was there to hear. He went over to his side table an took last year's Christmas card from Maria out of the drawer. She sent a picture every year of the family as a Christmas card along with an update of the family's year. Tony held the card up like he was examining a valuable artwork. Maria had a nice-looking family. Even Frank, who he was not fond of, cleaned up pretty well. He pulled out the letter and reread it. It was getting a little worn from the reading. The family had a good year last year. Both kids were involved in sports. The youngest one started Tee ball. Frank liked his job at the machine shop. He was promoted to foreman. Their church group did a service project in Dayton. They build a playset in a park for under privileged kids. Tony took along sip from his beer. He was missing so much, and he wanted to be there.

CHAPTER 24

A BABY

"Tony Sincero dial 5015"

"That's a different number" Tony thought.

"Hi This, is Tony Sincero, you paged me?"

"Yes Tony, this is Brenda in H.R. we just got a call from the hospital. They couldn't get ahold of you. Your wife has just been admitted in labor"

"Labor? what do you mean? She is not due for two more weeks"

"We just know what they said"

"Thanks"

Tony grabbed his coat and his brief case and started for the door in a trot. Guido saw him running by.

"Where are you off to in such a hurry?"

"Labor" Tony said one word and kept going. Guido made a puzzled look over at Alice.

"His baby is coming" She said.

"And he needs to be there? I wasn't here for mine"

"It's the twentieth century Guido, things have changed" then under her breath "Barbarian".

Tony whipped his car into the first parking space he saw at the hospital and barely remembered to shut it off when he jumped out. He ran through the front door and up to the reception desk. The receptionist looked at him. He was sweaty and flushed, breathing like a marathoner.

"Are you okay?"

"Labor"

"You're in labor?"

"No, my wife is in labor"

"Bring her in, I will get a wheel chair brought 'round"

"No, no she is already here"

"Oh, why didn't you say so- take the elevator to the third floor and follow the signs"

Tony pressed the button for the elevator and waited, anxiously, not patiently. He was running in place when the bell rang, and the door opened. He had to wait for someone to push someone in a wheel chair out first. "C'mon, c'mon" he was thinking. Finally, the elevator was empty he jumped in and pressed 'three' before anyone else could get in. It was the longest two-story elevator ride of his life. The door opened on the third floor and he saw a sign for 'maternity'. The maternity area was all the way to the end of the hall way. He was afraid the baby would be born before he got there. When he rounded the corner to the maternity ward the nurse at the station took one look at him and pointed him to a room. He went into the room. Madison was on the bed and a doctor was talking to her.

"Is everything alright?" Tony interrupted whatever was going on.

"Is fine, is fine" Said the doctor "your baby is just in a hurry to meet you. It won't be long now"

Madison looked up at Tony and made a slight smile. A contraction hit and her faced grimaced. Tony didn't know what to do. Six weeks of baby birthing classes went right out of his head. He gave her his hand. She squeezed it so tightly he thought his fingers would pop off. They actually turned purple.

"I am so glad you are here" Madison said between breaths.

"I would not miss this for anything"

"They said they couldn't find you"

"They did find me, and I am here now"

The nurse came in and did a check. She handed Tony some booties, a smock and a cap and said" It's time"

They rolled Madison into the other room and the doctor came in. After much hand squeezing and pushing the baby was born. It was a beautiful little girl. The nurse put the baby on Madison's chest and asked if they had a name for her.

"Maria. Maria Linda after her grandmothers"

"That's a pretty name. She's perfect"

After all was settled and Madison and Maria were moved back to a private room Tony went out to the lobby to make some phone calls. His mother-in-law was walking in.

"I was just about to call you"

"Is everything okay?" there was a bit of panic in her voice "I thought I would come to give you a break"

"Everything is perfect. You are a grandmother. You have a beautiful, happy granddaughter"

"May I see her"

"Of course,".

For the first time in the years he knew her Tony saw Madison's mother act like a nurturing human being. She completely dropped her patrician facade and wept as she held the baby.

"She's beautiful" was all she could say.

The nursery was already complete. They were not sure of the gender, so they went with muted yellow colors. Madison's parents insisted on buying the best crib and baby stuff money could buy. There was a mobile over the crib and a big stuffed bunny. They also bought a changing table and all the required diaper stuff. There was nothing for Tony to do here. Tony took the rest of the week and the next one off from work. He wanted to be home to help as much as he could.

Madison's parents also bought the latest and greatest in high tech baby car seats. Tony normally objected to their helping out but in the case he decided the baby was more important that his pride and he gracefully accepted all of their help. Tony mounted the car seat in the back of the Volvo and went to pick Madison and Maria up at the hospital. It took a while at the hospital to get the paper work squared away and finally it was time to go home. Madison wanted to walk out to the car. The nurse insisted she had to be brought out in a wheel chair.

"But I will be walking when I get home!" she complained.

"Sorry, it's the rules"

Before they could put the baby on the car someone from the hospital had to come out an inspect the car seat. More rules.

"This is very impressive" The hospital person was a car seat connoisseur. She knew a good one when she saw it. "This must have set you back a few bucks". Kind of rude of her to say but it was a pretty good car seat.

"Only the best for Maria" Tony politely replied.

Maria had quite a set of lungs on her and cried the whole way home. Madison was still exhausted and slept through it. When they got home, Tony picked Maria up out of her car seat and held her against his chest. She almost immediately stopped crying. Madison was impressed.

"You must be magic" she said.

Tony sat Madison down on the couch an gave her a blanket. Then he took Maria to her room and changed her diaper. It was the twentieth century, men did that. He held her for a while and she fell back to sleep. He laid her gently into the crib and stared for a while. When he got back to the living room Madison was asleep as well. "More magic" he thought.

"Can I have a cup of tea? There was no good tea in the hospital" Tony made two cups of tea. He liked his black and Madison like milk and a little sugar. He knew just how to make it. He brought the tea and a couple of sugar cookies into the living room.

"How are you feeling?" Tony asked Madison.

"Exhausted, it's good to be home"

"It's good to have you home".

The next week was both exhausting and exhilarating. Tony and Madison took turns getting up with the baby. Madison regained some of her strength. Somehow, they were managing to function on very little sleep.

The phone rang. "Is this Madison? Congratulations. It's Guido from Tony's work, is he around?"

"Yes, I will get him for you" cupping her hand over the phone "Tony- it's Guido"

"What the heck does he want"

"He didn't say"

Tony took the phone. "Hi Guido, what's up?"

"We have an issue with Plymouth Insurance. We need you to go down there. It's important"

"Guido, I am out for another week"

"This will only take a couple of days. We need you"

"Okay"

Madison only heard Tony's side of the conversation.

"I'm sorry, I have to do this. It's important"

"If you have to...." She made her best disappointment face, Tony knew she was not happy.

"I have to leave tomorrow but I will be back in two days, I promise"

"yup". Madison answered curtly.

"It's my job" Tony pleaded

"Yup"

CHAPTER 25

Tony met Jessica at the coffee shop. It was her day off. She went there anyway. It was early in the day and no one was in there. It was quiet enough to have a conversation. Someone was playing light new age-ish music on the piano. He wasn't listening to them, he was in his own universe. Tony noticed he was playing without shoes on. Now and then a melody Tony recognized with go by for a while the it would morph into another melody then some improvisation and another melody. The playing never stopped just flowed from melody to melody. Some Tony knew, some he didn't. Overall, he found it quite pleasant. He made a note to come back when the piano man was there. Tony was feeling pretty mellow.

"Did you call your daughter?" Jessica asked Tony.

"Yes, I did."

"How did it go?"

"Well....not well. She did not sound like she wanted to talk to me. She's holding quite a grudge that I apparently put on her shoulders"

"You can make it better"

"I don't think so. I was not there for her much when she was growing up. I was always working. I am afraid I didn't give her much by the way of nurturing. If I wasn't at work I was talking about work or recovering from work"

"Recovering from work?"

"We drank a bit at my job. You had to do it to keep up socially"

"Had to do it?"

"Oh yes, it was expected"

"Maria holds that against you?"

"I guess she does. I am not sure why"

"I think you know why"

Tony looked puzzled. He expected Jessica to be on his side. She was challenging him a little here.

"Maybe you drank too much?"

"I drink a lot, but I don't have a problem with it. I can stop any time."

"Okay, you can stop any time. Can you stop right now?"

"I could but I don't choose to. It's my one guilty pleasure"

"Tony, maybe you need to step back and take a look at yourself. I am not saying you are bad. You are one of the nicest guys I have ever hung around with. Your grand kids are growing up without you and it seems to me that the drinking has something to do with it."

"Have you been speaking with Maria?"

"No, I don't even know how to get ahold of her. I have seen this before. I think you need to get some help. Don't waste this."

"You don't know what you are talking about"

"Yeah, I do. Why do you think the kids live with me and not their mother?"

That wasn't what Tony wanted to talk about. As far back as he can remember, at least since he left college, he has always been able to hold his booze. Sure, it was a problem for some his coworkers and they had to fire the occasional one. It was never a problem for him. He resented Jessica implying that he had an issue. He changed the subject.

"Maria's husband is a machinist. We weren't, at least I wasn't, very enthusiastic about him at first. Madison had to remind me that her parents felt the same about me. He's a good man. He takes good care of her and the kids. He works hard. They don't have a lot of money, but they are not starving."

"What more can you ask?"

"True, what more is there really"

"How did they meet?"

"She was working as a temporary secretary and he worked in the shop. One night her car wouldn't start in the parking lot. He had just finished an over time shift and saw her with the hood up"

"Knight in shining armor then?"

"More like mechanic in greasy coveralls that happened to have jumper cables" He saw a slight smile go across Jessica's face.

"Did they start dating right then?"

"No, not for a while. She was interested in him, but he was too shy and intimidated to ask her out. They would pass in the building at work and make small talk, but he would never ask"

"What got him to ask?"

"She asked him. There was a concert she wanted to see, and she bought two tickets."

"That's sweet"

"They've been together ever since"

"Nice".

"I do wish I could get to know him and the kids better"

"You could. Maybe I can help"

"Will you talk to her?"

"I will but not right away.

The piano player took a break. Tony called him over.

"That is some sweet playing. Can I buy you a coffee?"

"Thanks, they give me free coffee here"

"Do they pay you?"

"Nope but there's a tip jar. I don't worry about it too much. I like to play, and I like to see people relax"

"If you got paid you could buy some shoes"

"I have shoes over there" the piano man points to the piano "I like to play without them. I can feel the music come up through my feet. The low notes anyway"

"Have you been playing long?"

"It seems like all my life."

"You are very good"

"You are too kind. I am glad you enjoyed it. I have to get back to work"

"Talk to soon"

"See you soon"

Tony turned back to Jessica

"What a nice guy, I envy the talent he has"

"Do you play anything?"

"A little bit of guitar but it has been a while"

"Bill and Charlie play bluegrass. Do you play that?"

"I know some of the songs, but I am not very good"

"Maybe you could get together with them. They are always looking for people to play with"

"I'd like that".

Tony met Bill and Charlie when he helped work on Anne's house. They were nice guys. He thought that it might be fun to get together with them.

Jessica said "I'll tell you what. I know they get together over at the church building on Saturday mornings. I'll bring you by"

"Thanks, that would be fun"

Tony decided that when he got home, he probably should put some new strings on his old guitar. The ones on there were about ten years old. He hadn't played it much since he used to sing lullabies to Maria when she was little. He wondered if she even remembered that.

.

CHAPTER 26

MARIA LEARNS TO DRIVE

"Driving lessons?" Tony asked.

"Maria wants to take driving lessons this fall"

"She is only...." Tony hesitated for a couple of seconds and did the math in his head. "Oh crap, she is sixteen"

"Yes, and she wants to learn to drive. You are never around to teach her."

"I am around, I can teach her"

"You are not around and when you are you are not in a condition to teach her. You are too impatient and sometimes, quite frankly, too drunk"

"I don't drink that much"

"Only on weekends, after work and when you are hung over" Madison was done pulling her punches.

"Let's not fight about this again"

"I am tired of fighting about this. You know what to do. Meanwhile I am getting Maria driving lessons"

Tony took his beer and went out to the porch. They bought this house about ten years earlier. Business was good, and he was making good money. His favorite feature was the porch. He could sit out there for hours reading and enjoying his scotch.

Maria came out to the porch "Hi daddy, mom told me about the driving lessons. Thanks"

"I could teach you myself, you don't need lessons from a stranger" Tony's ego was bruised.

"I want to take lessons. It will go faster. You don't have time"

"Do what you want". Tony was curt.

"Fine" Maria left a little sad. She got her driving lessons, but she could never seem to make her father happy. It seemed like he had been in a bad mood since she was seven. Maybe not seven but certainly for a long time. Maria felt like it was somehow her fault. He mother assured her otherwise.

"Why can't you be nicer to her?" Madison was standing at the door.

"I was nice, she is headstrong, I miss the little girl that hung on my every word"

"You were not nice. She looks up to you and worries that you don't like her"

"She's my daughter and I love her. I have a lot on my mind"

"Like what? It's Sunday afternoon. Relax."

"I have to lay off some people tomorrow and it will not be pleasant. Business has slacked off. One of them is Guido"

"Your old boss?"

"Yup, my old boss. I want to keep him around, but we just can't afford the luxury. He doesn't pull his weight anymore. The other day after lunch he slept at his desk most of the afternoon"

"After lunch? How many?"

"Two or three, that's not the point. I owe him, he mentored me. He hired me out of school. It's killing me to have to lay him off"

"Do you see your future at all?" Madison was blunt.

"What do you mean?"

"He was were you are at one time"

"Leave me alone". Tony opened his book and refused to talk any more. He was not ready for what he thought he had to do.

The next day Tony went onto work one big ball of nerves and terror. This was the day he had to let people go. He had one hundred people under him and had to lay off ten of them. He could delegate some of it to his section managers, but he felt he should do it himself. Most of the guys were pretty good at what they did and young enough to get new positions. He was most worried about Guido. Guido was getting close to the end of his career and getting a new position will be rough. Guido was once the star salesman in the company and could do no wrong. He was always a social drinker and good at schmoozing the customers. A few years ago, he lost his wife and his social drinking got to be more of a daily thing. After a while it affected his work. Tony didn't see it because he was Guido's drinking buddy and also felt like he owed Guido for all that he had done for him in the early days. Numbers don't lie though and when it was time to decide who to let go Tony's vice president put Guido's name on the top of the hit list. Business has no room for sentiment. Tony reached in his desk an got out his bottle of scotch. He poured a couple of fingers in his coffee cup and drank it down in one gulp. This was not sipping scotch. He called Guido to his office. Guido walked in and saw the orange folder on Tony's desk with his name on it. Tony poured him some scotch.

"I can't pretend I wasn't expecting this. I know things have not been great lately. I can turn it around though if you give me a chance."

"Guido, if it was my call you know I would give you all the chances you need. Another?" Tony topped off Guido's cup.

"Maybe you could go to management and plead?"

"That ship has sailed. This is what it is. You've been here a long time. You'll get the maximum severance which I think is eight weeks"

"Eight weeks? I have been here eighteen years!"

"I know, eight weeks is all they can afford. We will also give you a good recommendation"

"Eight weeks, sheesh"

"I need you to sign this and this" Tony put some papers forward. "They won't give you severance until you agree not to sue for age discrimination."

"I guess you guys have me by the shorts"

"Sorry, it's not my decision. Business is not good"

"I won't hold it against you. I have been in your shoes. Your expensive Italian backstabbing shoes" the scotch was kicking in.

Tony waved in the security guard. "This guy will help you with your stuff from your desk. Sorry"

"Kiss my ass" Guido walked out of the room for the last time.

Tony refilled his coffee cup from the bottle in his desk and leaned back in his chair. Nine more to go. Hopefully they go better than this he only had so much Scotch.

This was an absolutely horrible day for Tony. He had to lay off Guido, his original mentor, two guys with pregnant wives, one young woman who started crying before he could finish the speech, two guys who gave him the finger on the way out and one guy who was going to quit anyway and was all excited trying to think of how he would spend the severance pay. By the end of the day he was wishing it was he who was getting laid off.

On the way out, he walked by Guido's office. It was almost empty. All that was left was a picture of Guido, Mike and Tony having a drink right after they closed on that bank deal that was his first big deal. Guido didn't take that with him. Tony picked it up and stared at it for a minute. They all looked so young. Mike was gone now, and he had to lay off Guido, Alice moved to Florida a few years ago. No one was left from the old days. He stuck the photo in his brief case. Maybe Guido would want it back someday.

CHAPTER 27

JAMMING

Saturday came around and true to her word Jessica brought Tony over to the church building to meet with Bill and Charlie. Tony is what is commonly referred to as a recovering Catholic. He was used to ornate formal churches with art and statues and stained-glass windows. You wouldn't play bluegrass in the sanctuary of a Catholic church building. The church Bill and Charlie belonged to was a small community church. The building could have been any type of meeting hall. There was no ornateness, no statues that looked at you with imploring eyes that seem to say, "what did you do to me?" It was a simple room with a few folding chairs and a table. Bill and Charlie were tuning up. Bill had a Martin D28 and Charlie had some kind of Mandolin Tony didn't recognize the make. Tony wasn't up on his Mandolins.

"Hey Tony, how are you doing?" Bill greeted Tony like an old friend.

"I am okay. A little nervous. I haven't done this in a long time"

"Don't worry. It's all for fun. We will play mostly three or four chord songs. Watch me and you'll pick up on it quickly"

Tony had a reasonably good ear. He should be able to pick up on a simple song. He sat across from Bill, so he could see what he was playing.

Bill looked over at Charlie and said, "Sunny Side in G" and launched into "Keep on the Sunny side". Tony watched Bill's hands and by the third verse had picked it up pretty well. Charlie took a solo then Bill took one. Tony did not feel comfortable soloing, he was just barely getting the chords, so he passed. The three of them played a bunch of songs and tunes together. Charlie was a pretty good mandolin player. He knew a lot of fiddle tunes. Tony really enjoyed one called "Saint Anne's reel".

Bill said "You guys want to take a break and get some coffee?"

Tony and Charlie both said, "Good idea".

There was a small kitchen area and there was already a pot of coffee brewing. They each grabbed a cup and sat down.

Tony asked, "Do you guys want anything to spice that coffee up?" He had a bottle in his pocket.

"No thanks" replied Charlie, "we both have issues with that kind of thing, so we stay away for it. Feel free yourself though"

Tony didn't feel right about going ahead. "I'll pass too in that case"

"Your call. Booze has gotten me in more than my share of trouble. I stay away from it now. It took a long time to get here" Bill said.

"I really appreciate you guys letting me jam with you. It has been a long time since I picked up the guitar. My fingers are killing me. No callouses"

"You did well Tony, we enjoyed having you"

"Yeah, keep coming back it was fun. I heard you harmonizing on a couple of those songs. you were good" Charlie added.

"I didn't know what I was doing I just did what I thought sounded good"

"It did sound good."

Tony did not even notice Jessica had left until she came back in the door. She was out back with the kids. They were playing on the swings. Churches didn't have swings when Tony was growing up.

"Did you have fun?" Jessica asked.

"I did, thanks for bringing me, Can I ask you a question?"

"Sure"

"Both these guys said they had issues wth the booze in the past, but they seem pretty together now. How did they do that?"

"Are you interested in doing the same?"

"I don't think that I need to I was just curious"

"There's a program at this church"

"Like AA?"

"Not AA, a little different. It helped them and others"

"Maybe I could check it out? Not for me, I just want to see what it is about" Tony was starting to crack.

"You can, they are open to everyone. You don't have to participate you can be an observer. They meet on Thursday nights. I could bring you"

"I'll think about it"

Jessica dropped Tony off at his place. The kids had fallen asleep in the back seat of the car.

"Thanks again for bringing me"

"I am glad you had fun"

"See you soon"

Tony went inside, opened a beer and sat at his kitchen table. He was thinking about the jamming and and about Bill and Charlie. There was a time not long ago when he wouldn't have spent time with guys like Bill and Charlie. He would have considered them losers. They did not have a lot of money like he did back then and who quits drinking? Only losers can't handle their booze. he was practically professional at it. "Professional" he muttered. He took a long drink from his beer and put it down on the table. One-time Tony lived in a big house in a well to do neighborhood. His neighbors were lawyers and doctors. He drove nice cars and had money in the bank. Now he lived in this trailer with second hand furniture and an old car. No money in the bank. At least Madison still had some money in the bank. He didn't. He looks down at the kitchen table. It was pink formica. The edges were banded in metal and it had metal tubular legs. The color was worn off of the formica in places. This was his kitchen table. It wasn't cherry with burled walnut. It was formica and aluminum. His little propane cook stove was white porcelain and had two burners. His kitchen used to have a six-burner chef's cook top with a big overhead exhaust hood. His refrigerator used to be a big side by side with fancy digital controls and an ice maker. The fridge he had now belonged in a dorm room. "Professional" he thought.

Thursday rolled around, and Tony was sitting in his kitchen drinking his second cup of coffee. The last few days were kind of a blur. The sun came in through the kitchen window and Tony could hear Lorraine outside talking to her dog, Sparky.

"Sparky get over here. Don't go near that!"

Tony looked out the door and said, "What's your dog up to?"

"She keeps going through the trash over there. I think she smells meat"

"Don't you feed her?"

"I feed her plenty. I think that guy over there doesn't like her and puts poison meat in his trash"

"Do you know him? Does he know her?"

"I have no idea. Don't know him but he looks shifty. He could be a spy"

This was the same neighbor with the smug garden gnome. Tony was pretty sure he wasn't a spy. Tony saw him coming out in his ribbed tee shirt and boxers the other day to get his paper. If he's an undercover spy fifty pounds of overweight, balding, glasses, unshaven, wife beater tee shirt and boxers is a great cover.

"I don't think he's a spy Lorraine"

"He has a gun. I seen it"

"A lot of people have guns"

"He's a spy. Stay away from him"

"Ok, sure" Tony was pretty sure there were no national security secrets to spy out on the trailer park. Sparky ran over when he heard his voice and Tony petted her.

"Careful, she bites" It was the spy across the way.

"Not me" Tony was proud of that. He knew that she bit on occasion, but she never even nipped at him. He had a way with dogs and little kids.

A car pulled up. It was Jessica. She got out and walked over.

"So, who is this?" Lorraine was curious.

"Lorraine, this is Jessica, Jessica- Lorraine"

"Nice to meet you. The guy over there is a spy. Be careful"

"He's not a spy Lorraine" then to Jessica "Can I get you a coffee?"

"I could use a coffee"

"Great, come one in"

Tony poured a coffee for Jessica and one for himself. He was down to his last two clean coffee cups. he would have to wash some dishes soon. He had a dishwasher at his old place too. Not here.

"Have you given any more thought to dropping in on that recovery group tonight?" Jessica asked

"I have, I think I will do that"

"Bill and Charlie will be there, so you will know three people"

"Three people?"

"I will be there too"

"Are you recovering?"

"No but I hope to get my daughter in some day. It's for support and recovery"

"Okay, that's cool"

Tony was not convinced he needed the group, but he wanted to show Jessica he was open minded.

"Pick me up at seven and we will go over" Jessica said

"How about if I pick you up at six and we eat first?"

"Okay- see you then"

When Tony got to Jessica's place, he could not believe what he smelled. He could smell it before he even got to the apartment door. It smelled like home to him. It smelled like nurturing to him. It smelled like sauce. Jessica made some ziti with marinara sauce and it smelled just like his mother's sauce. Jessica opened the door and the joyful smell increased about ten-fold. Tony almost fell down the stairs with excitement. On the table were two big bowls of ziti, a big bowl of salad with olives, tomatoes, balsamic dressing and grated cheese There was a piece of Italian bread and a plate of oil to dip it in. The oil was very green. Tony could tell to was extra virgin olive oil. He noticed pepper and little bits of garlic floating in it. He was floored. Jessica was not even Italian.

"Wow, this is awesome" he could not hide his excitement "how did you learn to do this?"

"It's not hard. I grew up in an Italian neighborhood. My next-door neighbor was a sweet widowed lady that cooked like this all the time and taught me a few secrets. She lived to be one hundred and three, so I figured this was why"

"Thank you- this is great"

They sat down to eat. Jessica was very proud of how happy she was able to make Tony.

"Where's my little buddies?" he asked after the kids.

"Thursday nights they have supervised visitation with their mother"

"Oh, how does that work?"

"I drop them off at a volunteer's house and their mother meets them there. One of the people in the church is a social worker that facilitates such things"

"That's nice. You don't go?"

"Not yet."

Tony could tell that that was the end of that line of conversation.

"How does it work tonight?" he asked

"We will go t the meeting. You can sit anywhere you want. You don't need to talk you can feel free to just listen. The only rule is whatever is said there stays there"

"Like Vegas"

"Yeah, like Vegas" Jessica smiled.

Tony did not expect so many people. There were about fifty people in the hall when they got there. Tony recognized a couple from around town. "I wondered about him" Tony thought when he saw a guy, he used to see at the restaurant but hadn't seen in a while. Bill and Charlie were sitting off to left. Tony and Jessica joined them.

"Nice picking the other day Tony"

"Thanks Bill, I enjoyed it."

"Lets's do it again".

A gavel banged across the room and in startled Tony. He jumped a little.

"Time to start" Charlie whispered.

"Good evening everyone. Welcome. I see a lot of familiar faces here and a few new ones. Let me review the group rules. This is a judgement free zone, only helpful comments please. Only speak when you have the talking stick or have been called on to ask a question. Above all whatever is said here stays here. Nothing leaves this meeting. There is also no business taking place here. No schmoozing you sales guys" some folks chuckled. "Okay - Who wants to start?"

Someone across the room raised his had. He was a little younger than Tony, dressed casually on jeans and a golf shirt. He stood up and started speaking.

"Hi everyone, I'm Tom"

"Speak up" said half the room in unison.

"My name is Tom. This is my second visit here. I do pretty well most of the time. My biggest problem seems to be work. The guys I work with like to go out after work and toss a couple back. If I go with them, I end up being the last guy to leave every night. It is starting to cause issues at home. What do you guys do about this?"

"The obvious solution is to avoid hanging out with the guys after work. At least until you get this under control." The moderator spoke up.

"I would do that but some days I carpool, and my ride goes out too"

"Why don't you offer to be the designated driver those nights?" someone on the other side of the room offered.

"That's a good suggestion. If you can't remove yourself from the situation at least give yourself a reason to not participate" The moderator suggested. "Of course, the best thing is to avoid temptation all together"

The conversation went on on this way for another hour. Guys, and it was mostly guys, would get up and pose a question or relate a problem. The moderator or one of the other participants would offer a suggestion and help. Tony was surprised at how open everyone was. Being raised in an old world and Catholic environment he was not used to people sharing such intimate details.

Jessica asked, "What did you think of the meeting?"

"It was a little uncomfortable for me. I kept thinking there was too much information being shared. I didn't want to know some of those things. That guy with the wife in jail, I didn't need to know why. I might have to wash my brain when I get home"

"That's how it works. It's a support group. You can't support someone if you don't know what's broken"

"I don't know...."

"You'll see"

Tony dropped Jessica off at her place and went over to The Embers. No one was in the bar. Tony took his customary seat at the end. He was happy to see Danny was working that night. He liked Danny.

"What can I get you Tony?"

"Bud light, I'm on the wagon" They both laughed.

"Danny, do you think I drink too much?"

"Too much for what?"

"Too much. "

"You're here a lot. I've seen worse" Danny refilled Tony's glass. A woman walked in to the room and sat at the other end of the bar as far from Tony as possible. She had tight red jeans on and her hair was an unnatural bleached blond color. There were a lot of hard miles on her. She was pretty close to her 'sell by' date. He recognized her as the "had to get something from my car" woman. He sat with his beer eating pretzels. The news was on the TV in corner. He pretended to be watching that.

"Hey- you're the double naught spy guy! I remember you" the woman yelled from across the room. She was loud, the kind of loud were you knew she did not know how loud she was. She had clearly been to a bar before she came there.

"I don't think so" Tony pretended not to know. The last time he saw her he told he used to be a spy and made up all sorts of adventures. She knew even then he was lying. He didn't even remember most of what he told her. He did remember trying to get her out to his car and her disappearing.

"Yes, you are" She picked up her drink walked over and sat next to Tony. She leaned in real close and spoke right into his face. Tony imagined her eye veins were some sort of street map. "You are such a liar"

"Look, I am sorry about that. I might have had too much to drink that night." Judging by how she looked now and how he remembered her he definitely did have too much to drink that night.

"You lied to me then you took off on me!" Her face was close, and she was spitting a little as she spoke. It was gross.

"I didn't take off on you, you took off on me"

"I went to the lady's room and when I came back you were gone"

"You said you were going to your car"

"Did I? Hmmm"

Danny waved Tony over to the other side of the bar.

"Excuse me" Tony went over to see what Danny wanted.

"Tony be careful with her. I think I remember that night. We found her passed out in the stall when we were closing up. We had to have the cops come and take her in. I almost lost my job for over serving her. I only served her a couple, but I guess she had a few before she got here"

"Thanks Danny" Tony went back to his seat.

"So, tell me all about being a spy, how was Liechtenstein?"

"I'm sorry, I was never a spy. I was a salesman and now I am an unemployed salesman"

"I knew you were a liar! Buy me a drink, you owe me"

Tony gestures to Danny for another round. He brought Tony a beer, but he only brought soda water for the woman.

"What's this crap!" she exclaimed" There's no vodka in here!"

"That's right, I am shutting you off you have had too much" Danny was standing his ground this time.

The woman got off the bar stool and stood on the deck of the Titanic. At least she was wobbling like she was on the deck. She picked up Tony's beer, poured it out on the floor, and threw the empty mug as hard as she could at Danny. Danny dunked down, and the mug smashed three bottles on the shelf behind him. She was reaching for something else to throw when Tony grabbed her arm and held it behind her. With her free arm she swung around and hit him square in the eye. He tried to restrain her, but it was liking holding on to a raging pit bull. She was amazingly strong. She pushed Tony away and he hit his head-on the pool table. Danny reached behind the bar for his stick. Two policemen were across the street at the gas station filling their car. One of the waitresses from the restaurant saw the commotion in the bar and ran out to get them. They came in just as Danny was winding up with his stick and Tony was trying to grab the woman. Danny saw them and quickly put the stick away. Tony didn't see them, and he sprung on the woman to tackle her. The two cops only saw Tony and thought he was assaulting her. They jumped in and each grabbed an arm. Tony heard his right shoulder pop. "Interesting" he thought "What was that noise?" Then a wave of pain over took him. He dropped to his knees with both cops still holding on to him. The woman spotted an opportunity and wound up to hit him in the face with a beer mug.

"Let him go- he was just trying to help. She's the one causing all the trouble" Danny pleaded with the cops.

"Yes, please let me go" Tony was seeing stars at this point.

The two cops dropped Tony rather unceremoniously to the ground and approached the woman. She stopped what she was doing and glared at them.

"Put the mug down and calm down" They told her. Slowly she put the mug she was holding on an empty table and stood up.

"How much have you had to drink tonight?" they asked her

"Not enough, that guy would not serve me" She pointed to Danny.

"I think you have had more than enough" the cop said

"None of your business, don't you have ticket to write or something? Don't you have to sell tickets to the policeman's ball? Get lost Barney Fife" Her speech was slurred.

"Ma'am, we have to take you in for your own good" She started swinging at them and it took both of them to restrain her. They got her hands behind her back and put the cuffs on her. Not really cuffs, zip ties. They turned their attention to Tony. Between the hit on the head, the dislocated shoulder and a few too many Tony did not look good either.

"Sir, we are going to have to charge you with interfering with police officer and drunk and disorderly conduct"

"I didn't do anything, ask Danny"

"He was just defending himself" Danny spoke up.

"We are taking them both in"

"What about my shoulder?"

"After you see the judge"

Tony spent the night in the jail cell with a dislocated shoulder and a splitting headache. The next day they brought the captain over to see him. The didn't get his shoulder treated and he wasn't able to clean up. He looks like death warmed over.

"My men told me about last night. We are going to do you a favor and not follow through on the charges but don't let us see you again"

They escorted Tony to the front door and dumped him on the side walk as is. Its as a long walk to his car an the was still in a fair amount of pain. He didn't know what to do but to call Jessica.

"Tony, it's six in the morning-what do you want?"

"I am sorry to call you, I had no one else to call". He told her the whole story about the bar and the fight and the cops and his shoulder.

"Let me get dressed and get you. You are going to the hospital" Jessica put on some clothes and pick Tony up. They went to the emergency room and Tony got the shoulder looked at. The doctor was able to pop it in place and gave Tony a sling and a few pain pills.

"Thanks so much for helping me out"

"You're a wreck"

"I know. What a mess"

"Let me get you home, I have to go to work and you have to get cleaned up."

"Thanks, sorry"

"Don't be sorry"

"Sorry"

CHAPTER 28

MARIA GETS MARRIED

"She's too young to get married" Tony said.

"Tony, she's twenty. We were not much older when we got married" Madison was right, so was Tony.

"It is not right. What kind of future does this guy Frank have? What is he a machinist?"

"It's a skilled trade."

"She'll be working her whole life to help make ends meet. I wanted better for her"

"Funny, you are sounding just like my father when I married you"

"I am nothing like your father"

"No, you are not." Madison was sarcastic.

Madison and Maria planned an elaborate wedding which set Tony back three month's pay. They had the best caterer, the best wedding DJ and a function room at the fanciest country club around. Tony did not even belong to the country club. He had no time for golf. There were two hundred guests. Tony didn't know he knew two hundred people. They invited their friends, several relatives and Tony invited important business contacts. It was a big day. Tony spent most of the day buying drinks for his business contacts and schmoozing. By the end of the day Tony was pretty well in his cups.

The happy couple went off to change into their going away clothes and came back down to the hall to say their good byes. Tony insisted on making another toast. Madison and Maria tried unsuccessfully to talk him out of it. He stood up on one of the tables. He almost fell off trying to get up there. The best man was close by and grabbed his elbow to help him up.

"Ladies and gentlemen, most of you are ladies and gentlemen I am not sure about some of you" Tony's speech was very slurred. "Please join me in a toast to my lovely daughter and the bum she is marrying". Tony held his glass up in the air and a little sloshed out onto his tux. He would be paying to dry clean that. "I wasn't pleased with this when I heard, and I hope I was wrong." The toast went on for another five minutes and each minute saw Maria and Madison getting more and more embarrassed and angry. Just when he was about to finish his toast Tony lost his balance and fell off the table into the arms of the best man. The best man and one of the waiters carried Tony into the other room and laid him on the couch. There was dead silence in the room. The only sound was the ice sculpture fountain.

"I guess my Dad has had a little too much fun" Maria tried to put a good spin on things even though she wanted to crawl into a hole and die. "Thanks everyone for coming. Don't forget to take home your favors from the table"

"Where are you off to?" Someone in the crowd called out.

"Far away" Maria answered and laughed. "We are not telling".

"Enjoy it wherever you go" someone else yelled out.

"Thank you"

Maria and Frank went out to the car. The best man and the ushers went above and beyond with the car decorations. They wrote 'just married' and 'now they're legal' in shoe polish on the windows. They tied a bunch of beer cans to the bumper and balloons to the roof. They would have to stop and clean it up before they hit the highway. It did not matter what they did to the car Maria and Frank could not be any more embarrassed than they were a little earlier. As they drove off Maria look back at everyone but her dad waving them good bye. "Far away" she said, "Far away".

CHAPTER 29

LIGHT DAWNS

Tony's shoulder was killing him. He didn't want to take the pain pills. He didn't like the way they made him feel. He took a bottle of whiskey off the shelf and poured about three fingers in a glass. That should dull the pain a little. He held the glass to his lips and sipped the whiskey. He rolled it around his mouth a bit and swallowed it. He could feel the warmth in his body. His shoulder still hurt though. The whiskey did not make his shoulder better. He was about to take another sip. He held the glass to his lips and a spasm of pain ran through his shoulder and across his back. He dropped the glass and it broke spilling whiskey across the floor. Tony sponged the whiskey up the best that he could and got out a broom the clean up the glass. Sweeping with one arm was harder than he expected. After he cleaned everything up, he went to get another glass and some more whiskey. His shoulder spasmed again and he grabbed onto the counter to brace himself. "What am I doing?" He thought. It dawned on him how he got into this position. If he wasn't at the bar his shoulder would not feel this way. Tony closed the cabinet and sat back down. He didn't so much want whiskey any more. He didn't even want beer. Reality had come up from behind, flipped him around, and smacked him on the side of his head, he put his head in his hands and wept.

He called Jessica "Do you think the guys will let me join their recovery group?"

"I thought you didn't need that" Jessica didn't mean to sound snide.

"I thought so too. Now I am not as sure"

"It might be just the pain in your shoulder talking"

"I don't think so. I need to do something. The shoulder is just the latest problem"

"There's a meeting tomorrow night. I will bring you. Pick you up at six"

"Thanks, see you then"

Tony was waiting outside, clean, sober and anxious at six the next night. Jessica picked him up and they drove to the meeting. It looked like the same group as the last meeting but now Tony didn't see any losers.

"What happened to your arm?" Charlie spotted Tony when he came in the door.

"Just a little misunderstanding" he replied.

"You won't be playing for a while, bummer. A bunch of were getting together this weekend. Hey- why don't you come by and do some harmonies any way? It will be fun"

"Thanks for that invitation, I will do that". Tony was really beginning to like Charlie.

The moderator called the meeting to order with the usual introduction and rules. Several people spoke. Tony had a different perspective on what he was hearing this time. He listened closely to what they all had to say. He noticed many parallels between his life and some of theirs. One guy was a successful building contractor until he started losing contracts because he would get belligerent with some of his customers. There was another guy who was fired from his factory job for showing up to work under the influence. It took more that a couple times for him to get fired which surprised Tony until he thought back to all the times Mike, Guido and he would celebrate almost any victory at work in the old days. They never got fired. For the first time in a couple of years Tony didn't feel alone. He had not even realized how alone he was feeling until that moment. Other people fought the same fights as he and were able to look back at them. He raised his hand to speak.

"Hi, my name is Tony Si."

"No last names please" The moderator interjected.

"Tony. I was a very successful salesman in my previous life. I had a wife, a daughter, a big house and nice cars and I have come to realize I drank them away. For the longest time I blamed my wife, I blamed my boss, the economy, everyone but myself. Sitting here I understand that it wasn't any of those things it was me. It took broken shoulder and a hit on the head to do it. I know now it was me" There was a tear in Tony's eye. He wiped it away quickly before anyone saw. Someone came up behind him and put an arm around his shoulder. It was Bill. Jessica patted him on the back and they all sat down.

When Tony got home that night, he poured all of his whiskey down the drain and got the last six pack out of his refrigerator. He looked at it sitting on his table all nice and cold. "It's only beer" he thought "what could it hurt?". His shoulder chose that time to send a spasm of pain up to his brain. He took the six pack outside and tossed it onto the trash bin.

"Hey what are you doing?" Lorraine saw him do it.

"I don't need these anymore"

"I might, why didn't you give them to me?"

"You probably don't need them either"

"Hell, I don't" Lorraine went over to the bin and dug out the beers. She was sure she could wash the coffee grounds and whatever else was on the cans off.

"Hey- what happened there?" She was so concerned with the cans she did not notice the sling.

"I had a run in with the law" Tony repeated the whole story about the red jeans woman and the cops.

"You could sue"

"I won't. Its s my own fault"

"I'd sue"

"Thanks for the advice"

"Really you should sue. Call that lawyer I see on TV, Soko something"

"Sokolove"

"Yeah, whatever, he'll get you money. By the way speaking of money did you ever call that guy with the card?"

Tony had forgotten about the card. "No, maybe I should

"He looked like he had money"

"I doubt it, I had to fire that guy once"

"Oh oh- maybe he wants to get revenge"

"Maybe. Maybe I should just talk to him"

Tony went back inside and looked for the card. He hoped he didn't lose it. He hasn't been very organized lately. He found it under some magazines on his kitchen counter. It was a bent and had a coffee stain on it, but he could still read it. It scared the heck out of him to call that number. He wasn't sure what he was going to find on the other end. He had to at least apologize. He dialed the number.

"Hello"

"Guido, it's Tony. Tony Sincero."

"Tony!! How have you been? I dropped by your place a while back. Someone told me you moved there. I had a devil of a time tracking you down, what are you up to?"

"Listen Guido, I want to apologize for how things went the last day we worked together. I was a bit of a jerk. I owe you big time. You were my mentor and my friend, and I treated you like dirt"

"No, no, no don't apologize, I earned that lay off. I knew I wasn't producing. I was very angry that day but after a while things got better"

"What did you do?"

"For a while I sat home, watched daytime TV and drank. I did get married again too. I met her at unemployment and we hit it off. Then one day my wife had enough and said 'You have to do something else'. I tried a few things, selling cars, driving a cab, I even was a radio DJ once, nothing stuck until I ended up selling real estate. I realized I like interacting with people and selling them something they actually want to own. The money isn't what I used to pull in in the old days, but the pressure is a lot less. I am home a lot. My wife is pretty happy"

"You always knew how to sell"

"Yes, I did. I taught you! You didn't need much, you were a natural"

"I needed your help back then"

"The reason I tried to find you is this, I am opening my own real estate office and I heard you were unemployed, so I thought I would recruit you."

"I don't know real estate"

"You'll learn. Like I said, you are a good salesman. My only requirement is I have to keep an alcohol-free office. I hope you are good with that. We used to enjoy our tipple in the old days"

"I am more than good with that. Couldn't be better" Tony didn't think he needed to talk about the shoulder and the cops and the support group.

"Great, I will sign you up for the license course. Come by my office tomorrow and we will do the paper work. It will be great working with you again"

"Yes, thanks for this. I owe you again"

"Yes, you do "Guido laughed.

Guido's office was not very far from Tony's place. It was in a nice brick building next to the strip mall. Tony was sitting in the reception area. Guido came out of his office. He looked mostly the same as when Tony last saw him. His hair was shorter and grayer. Tony thought he actually might look younger even.

"You recognize Alice?" He didn't. Alice was older than he remembered. He pretended anyway.

"Wow, yes- how are you?" he held out his hand.

"I am well. Not bad for an old lady" Alice had to be in her seventies at least.

"Weren't you in Florida?" Tony asked.

"Too many old people, I was bored" Alice replied.

"You came back up here to work?"

"I'm Alice"

"Alice works for me part time to help keep the paper work under control. Come in and sit"- Guido added

Tony said his goodbyes to Alice and joined Guido in the office.

"You can't actually start selling until you get your license, there is a course at the Community College that starts next week so your timing is good"

"Thanks for this chance, my unemployment was about to run out and I don't have much in the bank"

"I think you will be good at this"

Guido gave Tony some forms to fill out and sign. They spent the rest of the hour reminiscing about the old days.

"Remember Porter? What ever happened to him. He wasn't a bad guy once you got past the bravado"

"Porter went to run the west coast office as you know. He was still there when the company imploded. He worked for a while with the guys that bought the remains. Last I heard he bought a vineyard"

"Anyone ever hear from Bob?"

"Bob was laid off a year after you and I heard he divorced his wife, or she divorced him, and he moved to a farm in up state New York. He was brewing beer that last I heard"

"Those were some great days. I miss some of them"

"Me too" Tony didn't miss the last few years of them though.

Guido and Tony shook hands and Tony headed home. He was ready for this new chapter. He started his realtor class that next week. It wasn't very hard for him and soon he was licensed. He couldn't wait to get to work. he couldn't wait to tell Maria he was working and maybe get to see his grandkids.

Tony was happy after seeing Guido. Things were finally looking up. If not up at least not totally down. He stopped by the mail box and picked up his mail. He hadn't done that for a few days, no one ever sent him anything but bills and ads. There was a letter post marked Memphis, He could tell by the writing it was from Madison. She wrote him now and then whenever she felt she needed to. Usually the letters were travelogues as if Tony really cared at this point where she had been. The last one was about six months ago. Tony was feeling good and did not want to read it. He did not want to waste a rare feeling good moment. On the other hand, he had nothing pressing to do and he had to read it eventually, so he opened the letter read it.

Dear Tony:

I am writing you from a little town outside of Memphis that I am sure you have not heard of. How are you doing? I don't know why I asked, you won't answer. I have been well. I felt like I needed to tell that I've met someone. Actually, I met him last Christmas. He lives out this way and we have been seeing each other long distance for a while. We got married last weekend ....

The letter went on to say how wonderful everything is and how great this new guy, a car salesman, is and how happy they are blah blah blah. Tony tossed the letter on the pile of other letters Madison sent him over the last few years. He automatically headed for the cabinet to get his whiskey then he stopped and mumbled a little thanksgiving prayer that the whiskey was somewhere in the sewer system by now. Instead he poured himself some coffee. He sat staring at the pile of letters for few minutes mulling over the old days. He started spinning back down the mental path of second guessing all of his decisions since grad school. He knew there was stuff he could have done better. Barring inventing a time machine there was not a lot he could do about that now. Slowly, deliberately, he stood up, straightened his shirt and put his coffee cup down. He took the pile of letters and some old photos he was keeping with them, put on his hat, and went outside. There was an old steel bucket out by the side of the trailer that someone left there. Tony put the photos, the letters and some lighter fluid in the bucket and lit everything up. As the letters burnt away Tony could feel himself feeling lighter. He went back inside to get his keys and drove over to the coffeeshop.

Jessica was working the counter when he got there. As soon as he walked in the door, she poured him a cup of coffee and got a chocolate chip cookie out of the display case.

"How did you know?" He asked.

"You had that look"

"That look?"

"The 'I need coffee and cookie' look, I am a pro I know it when I see it" Jessica smiled.

"Well then, thanks. Do you have a minute? When's your break?"

"I can take a break now- you are the one one here excluding laptop guy" Jessica nodded over toward a young guy in suit sitting at one of the tables with an empty cup completely engrossed by whatever was on his laptop screen.

"Great, let's talk". Tony and Jessica sat on the couch at the end of the room. "I got a letter from Madison today"

"You haven't heard from her in a while, is everything okay?"

"Yes, she got married"

"Wow, how do you feel about that?" Jessica's voice betrayed a tiny bit of jealousy.

"Not the way I thought I would. A few months ago, it might have made me depressed. Now not so much."

"Have you given it a lot of thought?" Jessica asked.

CHAPTER 30

GETTING A RIDE HOME

Tony woke up on the couch with some one poking him on the head. He opened his eyes and it took a while to get them to focus on anything. Slowly a face came into focus. It was a kind face. It was looking at Tony like one would look at a hurt animal, part concern, part empathy and a small part of revulsion. It took Tony a while to realize it was the manager of the country club. He must still be in the country club he thought. The manager had a thick accent that Tony could not quite pin down. It sounded vaguely eastern European but also had a slight amount of New England cadence.

"Sir, Sir.. . Mr. Tony are you alright? You have to get up you can't stay here"

"Uh, uh wha? What time is it?"

"Mr Tony it is six in the morning. You have been on this couch all night. We need you to go. We have another function to set up for. "

"I have been here all night?"

"Yes, Mrs. Tony said to just leave you there"

"Is she still here, where is everyone?"

"Everyone left hours ago. Your party was over"

"Do I have a car here?"

"We will get you a ride home. Pierre can drive you" Pierre was standing over by the door. He was a young man about twenty or so. From his dress Tony assumed he must be a maintenance guy.

Tony got up off the couch and immediately fell back onto it. The room spun around, and his head hurt. The manager and Pierre grabbed his arms and helped him to the bathroom. Tony splashed water on his face tried to smooth his bed head, well couch head, hair with his hand. He was still wearing his tux and by the looks at it he was not going to get his deposit back. Pierre helped Tony out to his car. Pierre drove an BMW X5. "Nice car for maintenance guy" Tony thought. Tony's head was starting to clear a bit.

"I like this car"

"Thanks, I just got it. I needed a car that could sit more than two people" Pierre laughed.

"Have you worked at the country club long?"

"You might say so. I started as a caddy when I was fourteen"

"Are you a greenskeeper now? What do you do there? Just guessing by your dress"

"Not quite. I kind of own the place. My Dad started it"

"Sorry, I didn't know" Tony was a little embarrassed.

"Why should you? It's our family business. The manager is my Uncle Pete, my mom does the books and you met my sister when you booked the room"

"Who about your Dad?"

"He passed away a few years ago."

"Sorry to hear that"

"Thanks. Is this your house? Nice"

"Thanks, we moved here ten or so years ago."

Tony shook hands with Pierre and thanked him for the ride. With his coat over his shoulder and his tail between his legs he walked up to the front door. Madison opened the door just before he got to it.

"You look like crap"

"Thanks, I wasn't sure" Tony was a little snide.

"Get cleaned up, we need to talk."

"Okay."

Tony went up to his room, shaved and showered. He put on some clean clothes. He was feeling better already. When he got back downstairs Madison was sitting at the kitchen table with a cup of coffee.

"Coffee?" she asked.

"Can I get a little hair of the dog?"

"Coffee" She was adamant.

"Okay Coffee, thanks"

Madison poured Tony a cup of black coffee and sat down across the kitchen table from him. The kitchen was her domain. Not that she did all the cooking. Tony did some. Mostly pasta and sauce and maybe the occasional cannoli. He had a piece of broom stick for wrapping the cannoli dough before he deep fried it. It was a trick he learned from his mother. Madison had it in her head that she wanted the kitchen a certain way and Tony left it all up to her when they remodeled. There was a big island with a butcher block top that was good for rolling out dough to make breads and pastries. She put in a double oven on the wall with convection. There was a six-burner gas cook top to the left of the ovens with a big range hood vented directly outside. The counter tops were black granite and the cabinets were maple. There was a big water spigot over the cooktop for filling pots. Tony liked this kitchen too.

"We need to talk about yesterday." Madison's voice was just a little venomous.

"I know, I'm sorry. I got carried away"

"Carried away? You were hammered!"

"I was the bride's father I had to have a drink with my guests. It's tradition"

"You had more than a drink"

"I know"

"Do you understand how that made Maria feel? You ruined the best day of her life so far"

"Don't be so over dramatic, it wasn't that bad"

"Do you need to see the video?"

"Sorry, what do you want me to say?"

"I want you to say you are going to get some help"

"I don't need help!" Tony stomped out of the room.

Madison sat in the kitchen and watched the trees blow around outside the window. Her coffee had gotten cold and she debated making more. The amount of work it required to make more coffee was more than she thought she wanted to do just now. She decided she needed a walk instead. She put on her shoes and grabbed her coat off the rack. It was nice and sunny out, a little cool. She might not need the coat, but she took it anyway.

They lived in what people called an 'executive neighborhood'. The houses were all set back from the street. Everyone had at least three stalls in their attached garage, everyone's landscaping was perfect. No one did their own, they had a 'lawn man' for that. Madison grew up in such a neighborhood. She walked down the street past the big houses with nice yards. There were no yard ornaments, no garden gnomes or gazing balls, that was prohibited by the home owner's association. She did not know the neighbors very well. They only spoke casually when they ran in to each other and met once a year to do association business. Tony always said he didn't want to be too friendly with the neighbors cause 'then they want to borrow stuff'. Tony grew up in a tight knit neighborhood where everyone knew everything about everyone else. The kids wondered in and out of each other's houses at will. The fathers often borrowed stuff from each other without even asking. It was very communal. Tony didn't want a close neighborhood even after growing up in one. She wished she could know her neighbors better.

When Madison and Tony first moved to this neighborhood, they were so excited. It was their dream house. Tony worked hard and got a lot of bonuses. They were finally able to afford to live here. They didn't have enough furniture when they first moved in and Madison had a lot of fun furnishing the place. After they were there for a month or two and had a reasonable amount of decorating done, they threw a big party to meet the neighbors. Tony made a big impression, he and a couple of the neighbor men drank quite a lot and decided to relive their college days by playing touch football out on the street. Tony had his first ever ride in an ambulance.

She turned the corner onto the next street. There was a yellow house there that belonged to a young couple that owned their own business. She knew them from the home owner's association. They were nice people. Tony wanted to have them over for dinner sometime.

Sometimes a woman must take a lonesome walk when she has a lot on her mind. Madison walked for about two hours that morning. She had a lot on her mind. She lost count of how many times Tony promised to straighten out. She lost track of the excuses. There was always a work thing or a friend to console or a sports victory. It seemed Tony always had an excuse to drink. She had grown tired of it. She wasn't sure she even still loved him. Her mother's words from long ago kept echoing through her head. Maybe she was right. Madison reached into her pocket and pulled out a business card. It was the lawyer her friend had recommended a few months ago. The card had become pretty beaten up, but she could still make out the number. She pulled out her phone and dialed. She made an appointment for the following Tuesday. She kept walking until she was back to her house. She already started thinking of it as only her house.

Tony was sitting in the living room with a glass of scotch and a newspaper. He wasn't drunk yet, but he wasn't totally clear either. Madison didn't need another straw but if she did, he just provided one. He looked up from his paper.

"Hi"

"Hi, we have to talk"

"Go ahead, talk" Tony was borderline belligerent.

"You need to move out"

"For how long?"

"I don't know. Maybe for good"

"Why?"

"You know why. I can't deal with this any longer. You've been promising to change for years and you haven't"

"That's not fair, I have pressures and responsibilities"

"I have had quite enough. I am going up north for a couple of days and when I come back, I expect you to be gone"

"Give me another chance" Tony pleaded

"I've already called a lawyer"

"C'mon..."

Madison looked at him, turned, and walked away. She went upstairs and packed a bag. She decided she would go to Freeport and shop.

Tony sat in the living room and finished his scotch. "What can I do now?" he thought. He had no clue. He could get his own lawyer and fight this, that's what he could do. He went through scenarios in his head. They all ended in psychological blood shed. He was tired. He was broken. He decided to not fight it.

Madison's lawyer and Tony's lawyer got together and ironed out an agreement. Tony got to keep his motorcycle collection. Madison got the house and most of the retirement fund. It didn't seem fair, but Tony's lawyer assured him he couldn't do better. It was this or Tony pays alimony for the next twenty years. Since the lawyer knew Tony was about to lose his job, he recommended against that. Madison did not know Tony was about to lose his job, he hadn't told her. When it rains it pours and pours.

Tony had three days to figure out what to do. He could couch surf but guests and fish both stink after three days and in his case, he had ticked his friends off enough to be four days in before he even started. That was out. He rented a room at the extended stay hotel near home while he looked for a place of his own. He could only afford this for a short while. He boss had given six months to find another job. That was three months ago. Time was getting short. Luckily, he was able to find a guy to buy his three motorcycles. That put about forty K in his bank account.

Tony met with a real estate agent to show him some rentals. He wanted to move into one of the renovated mills up in Lowell and live a bohemian existence. He liked the idea of being near to the bones of Kerouac. The broker brought him to a place by the canal. It had a lot of exposed brick and stainless steel every where. The big windows had no shades. Tony didn't like that. The old wooden floors creaked as he walked over them. Not in an annoying way, more in a musical way. The developer had preserved the old freight elevators from the mill days, at least the appearance of them, he had to modify them for safety. The original elevators ran on a belt and pulley system. The big mill wheel in the basement would turn shafts on every floor to power the looms and equipment. The elevators originally were powered by one of these shafts. To move the elevator, you had to pull on a wire rope that hung in the shaft and move a belt from the neutral wheel to one of the power wheels. Which wheel depended on which way you wanted the elevator to go. When the elevator got to you you would pull the wire rope to move the belt back to the neutral wheel and stop it. There was a ball fastened to the wire rope and little clamp thing on the elevator meant to keep someone else on another floor from moving the elevator while you were loading or unloading it. Needless to say, this was not always reliable. Many a mill worker came close to falling into the shaft while loading an elevator. Fortunately, the elevators were pretty slow. The elevators in this building were left to look as original as possible but had been updated to the latest electronic elevator control to remove some of the adventure from riding the elevator. Tony liked the building and the location.

Next the broker brought Tony to an old victorian in the part of town where all the mill owners had once lived. These were nice old mansions. In their day they were the equivalent of Tony's 'executive neighborhood'. Now days they were a little worse for age and most of them had been subdivided into three or four units. He showed Tony an apartment on the top floor of one of these. It had a turret on one corner of the house and Tony's apartment would have a sitting area in the turret. Tony liked this place too, but it had no air-conditioning.

Finally, the broker took him to a town house style apartment near the highway. It had no personality and seemed very noisy. Also, no air-conditioning. They went back to the real estate office.

"So, what did you think?"

"I liked the mill best"

"I thought you would" he quoted Tony a rent.

"That's quite a bit more than I wanted to spend"

"I can get you the place in the house for a little less"

"How much less?"

The broker quoted a price that was still higher than Tony hoped but he was desperate. "Okay, lets' do the paper work"

"They will want to do a credit check and a background check. you will need to deposit two months rent ahead as well"

"We can do that" Tony signed the papers and went back to his hotel room "I've got that done at least" he thought.

Tony's lawyer called him to come and sign the final paper work for his divorce.

"That was quick" Tony mumbled.

"You didn't fight hard" the lawyer replied.

"Should I have?"

"That's your call"

"You're my lawyer, you should advise me"

"I did what I could. I was able to get you a little more money from your retirement account. She just wanted to get it over with too"

"Thanks" Tony replied. I will be over a little while. Tony went to the lawyer's office and signed the papers. His hand shook a little. He remembered what his mother said a long time ago about Madison not being 'one of us'. That made him wonder if he had married an old-world woman would he be signing these papers now. "Can't think like that" he muttered to himself.

"Did you say something?" his lawyer asked.

"No, no" his voice trailed off like he was falling away, maybe even down a cliff.

The lawyer took all the papers and counter signed them. He put them neatly into a manilla folder and handed them to his paralegal. "We'll file these on Monday and you'll get a check next week. We will take our fee out of that"

"Thanks" Tony turned and walked out. Partly he felt relieved. Partly he felt like a boxer who had taken too many to the head but hadn't fallen down yet. He decided. that he needed a drink. There was a cocktail lounge attached to the restaurant down the street. He decided to stop there.

He walked through the restaurant to the bar area. it was mostly empty. There was dark fake mahogany panelling on the walls that Tony figured was there since the fifties. He noticed a pool table in the center of the room and a dart board off to the side. The booths and the bar stools were clad in red naugahyde. "What the hell is a Nauga?" he asked himself. He strolled to the far corner of the bar and took a seat.

"What can I get you fella?" The bartender asked.

"Beer in a bottle, how about Bud?"

"You got it champ"

"You can call me Tony"

"You can call me Danny. Are you new in the area?"

"No, been here for years. I just left my lawyer and I decided I needed a drink" Tony was surprised he was even that forthcoming with his problems. Danny had the bartender knack. He brought Tony a Bud in a bottle and an empty glass to pour it in. Tony held the glass up to the light and looked at it. It wasn't dirty like he first thought. It was old and clouded up though. Tony poured the beer in and took a long swig.

"I'm guessing bad news at the lawyer"

"Divorce"

"My friend got one of those, most expensive thing he ever bought"

"You got that right, now I need to find a place to live"

"My friend has a trailer for sale down the street. He's moving to Florida. He only wants fifty K"

"Really? I'll think about it" Tony wasn't going to think about it. He didn't think he was that desperate.

"Here's his number if you are interested" Danny wrote a name and number on a card and handed them to Tony.

Tony ended up sitting there for another two beers before he switched to whiskey. Danny had one of the buss boys drive him back to his hotel room.

Tony awoke to knocking on his door. It took awhile for the noise to work its way through the haze across his brain.

"Housekeeping"

"Can you come back later? I am not up yet"

"Sir it's already one o'clock. If we don't do it now, we won't be able to get to it"

"Fine, let me rest we can do it tomorrow"

"Okay, Si."

"I have to get a place" he mumbled to himself. He put a pillow over his head and rolled over to go back to sleep. When he finally did awake up, he noticed had had two missed calls and a message on his cell phone. It was the real estate broker.

"Tony, give me a call". Tony would have appreciated a little more detail that that. He called the broker.

"It's Tony"

"Hey Tony, thanks for calling. The landlord for that apartment got back to me. It's a no go"

"Why?"

"Your credit report came back, and your credit rating is not high enough for him and I guess he found a drunk and disorderly charge you had"

"That charge was dropped, it was a whole misunderstanding and my credit is just tanked because of the divorce right now"

"Either way, he doesn't want to rent to you"

"What can we do?"

"We will have to lower our bar and look at less desirable locations. I know a couple of guys that won't do background or credit as long as you have the deposit"

"Okay, can you show me some places today?"

"Can you come by at two?"

"Yup- hey I don't have my car here can you pick me up?"

"Okay, see you then".

The broker showed Tony five or six places. When you lower the bar as far as he figured Tony needed to you are not looking at the Taj Mahal. Tony was starting to get pretty depressed. He had the broker drop him back at the restaurant, so he could pick up his car. "Might as well have drink" he thought.

"Hey, it's you again"

"Yes, it's me again" Tony admitted. Danny put a beer down on the bar without either one of them mentioning it.

"How's your day?"

Tony told Danny about the apartment hunting and the places he is down to looking at.

"You should check out my buddy's trailer. He needs to move this month and he is not asking a lot"

"I will do that'" Tony capitulated.

"Great, I'll call him" Danny went back to the bar and picked up the phone. Tony had no idea he meant he would call him right now.

"He's on his way over. The place is only less that two miles from here. His name is Jim".

Tony drank the first beer and Danny got him another. Jim came in the door.

"Hey Jimbo!" A big man in a sweatshirt and jeans came in through the door. There were what Tony hoped were ketchup stains on his sweatshirt and his hair was slightly unkempt.

"Jimbo, this is Tony, he might be interested in buying your place" Tony didn't get a chance to protest that he was just thinking about it.

"Hi Tony, my name is Jim. My friends call me Jimbo for short. You can call me Jimbo. You want to come over and see the place?"

"Hi Jim, uh Jimbo, sure when?"

"Let's go. My truck is outside"

Tony followed Jimbo outside to an old green Ford F150. The windshield was cracked and the front fender a little rusty. Tony noticed a 'rejected' sticker where the inspection sticker belonged. The bed was all scratched up and dented. Of course, it had a trailer hitch. "This is a working truck" Tony thought. Jimbo slid into the driver's seat.

"Just throw that crap on the floor" he said gesturing to the assorted pile of debris on the passenger seat. Tony jumped in and they drove off. Tony was still struggling with the seat belt when they took a left into the park. "Well, at least I didn't need it" he thought.

"So, you need a place?"

"I do"

"This is a great place. I wouldn't be selling it except my daughter moved to Florida and she has a little baby now. I want to move closer. You can have anything in the place you want too pretty much. I am only taking what I can fit in this truck"

After they pulled into the park, they took their second right. Tony noticed the name of the street was 'Madison'. "Great" he thought "this guy couldn't have lived on 'Broadway'". Jimbo pulled up next to a green trailer with an awning. They got out.

"Don't mind the lady next door, she's a little crazy but harmless. Believes in aliens" Jimbo said in a whisper pointing at the trailer next door to his.

"It's a little messy in here but you get an idea of what it is about. I will have it cleaned up before you move in" Jimbo opened the door and waved his arm like a circus ring master. The real truth was that compared with the rentals Tony was looking at this was a palace. It wasn't even all that messy. Tony was pretty surprised. Jimbo gave Tony the grand tour.

"This is the kitchen" Jimbo gestured with his left hand at the kitchen area.

"Down that way is two bedrooms and a can" Jimbo gestured with his right hand the other way.

"Take a look around, make yourself at home, Beer?"

"Sure, thanks"

Jimbo went to fridge and took out two Bud lights in cans and handed one to Tony. Tony took his and drank a big swig. he walked back to the bedrooms and the can and looked inside. On bedroom had a bed and a bureau in it. The other was just stacked with boxes. Jimbo was already packing. The bathroom had the usual toilet and sink and a standup shower. That was all Tony really needed.

"Danny said you wanted about fifty for it?"

"Fifty, I can go as low as forty-five"

"Fifty is okay" Sales man Tony could have negotiated him down to thirty-five or forty and left him feeling like he got a good deal. Broken Tony paid asking. "I will have my lawyer do the paper work if that's okay with you?"

"Fine by me, I just want to move soon"

"I will have him rush"

"Okay".

Tony surveyed his new palace. "Well, here I am" he thought.

CHAPTER 31

OHIO

Tony had been going to the recovery meetings pretty regularly and hadn't had a drink in weeks. It was time to call Maria. She told him one year, but he really felt like he was ready. He hoped she would give him a chance. For the first time, in he did not know how long, he prayed about it. He could almost hear God on the other end flipping through his book to remind himself who this stranger was. Tony wanted more than anything to see his grand kids, and Maria of course. The alcohol had fogged those feelings but now they were getting stronger by the day. He decided this would be the day he called her.

"Hello"

"Hi hun, it's your dad"

"Yes" Maria's voice was cold.

"I wanted to tell you how I have been" He went on to tell her all about the recovery group and Charlie and Bill. About his new job as a real estate agent and about Jessica.

"You've been faithful to the recovery group that long?"

"They're great guys. Bill and Charlie even have me playing the guitar again. They made me realize how much I was missing and how much I wanted to be normal and how much I wanted to be part of your life again"

"I need more than promises, you've made promises before" Maria was still skeptical.

"Can I at least be on probation?"

Maria cupped her hand over the phone. Tony could hear talking but it sounded like distant rumbling. He could not make out any words. After what seemed like an hour Maria came back on the phone.

"Okay, you are on probation. The first slip up and it's back to square one"

"Can I come out and visit?"

"Let me get back to you tomorrow"

"Fair enough, thanks"

Tony hung up the phone and did a victory dance across his little kitchen and to the fridge. He opened the fridge. There was no beer in there. There was no whiskey in the cupboard either. There was root beer though. Tony had taken a liking to root beer made with real sugar, not corn syrup. He took a root beer and his news paper and went to sit outside. It was a nice sunny day in about the high sixties. Tony sat under the awning and read the paper.

"Hey what are you doing out there?" It was Lorraine.

"Just reading the paper."

"Is that beer? I thought you quit. Did you give up on quitting?"

"Root beer Lorraine, root beer, and I am never going to give up on quitting"

"Good for you. I should do that some day"

"Why don't you?"

"I'm too old and set in my ways."

"You are not"

"Hey, did you hear about garden gnome guy over there" She decided to change the subject. "They took him away in the ambulance yesterday. I think he vapor locked"

"I hope he's okay"

"Me too, I wonder what his kids will do with his stuff. He's got a pretty nice TV. I can see it through his window"

"Lorraine, that's a little morbid"

"Just saying'"

"I might go to Ohio"

"Ohio? Is that where your daughter lives?"

"Yup, she will let me know tomorrow"

"Good for you, bring me back a buckeye"

"Do you even know what a buckeye is?"

"No but they got them there, bring me some"

"Okay Lorraine. A Buckeye"

Tony didn't know what a buckeye was either but if he saw one, he would bring to back for Lorraine. He hoped it would fit in his carry on.

Tony's phone started ringing, it was Jessica "Did you talk to Maria? Will you be visiting her?"

"Yes, I did talk to her. I hope to visit her. She is going to let me know" Tony sounded hopeful.

"Good luck with that. Let me know if I should talk to her"

"I will do that. See you later"

Tony spent most of the rest of the day cleaning up around the trailer. He had one house showing in the afternoon. It was a nice young couple that reminded him of Madison and him when they were starting out. He hoped he could find them a good place and that their luck was better than his. After the showing he stopped and ate at the new Sushi place that opened in town. He only recently started eating Sushi. He liked it. He was nervous about talking to Maria again, but he was excited about going out there to visit. He wanted to call her right now but knew he should wait for her to call.

Tony sat in his easy chair watching the news. The phone rang, and he picked it up. It was Maria! His stomach was doing back flips with anticipation and he had a lump in his throat.

"Hello Maria"

"Hi Dad. We talked it over and decided that we would like you to come out for a couple of days. We don't have a lot of room so, if you don't mind, could you stay at the hotel in town?"

"I would sleep in a cardboard box under a bridge if I had too!! When do you want me there? My schedule is pretty flexible"

"Can you come next Thursday and stay until Monday?"

"Yes! I'd love too. thanks", He could not have been happier. "See you then"

"We will pick you up at the airport in Dayton"

"Okay, can I bring the kids anything?"

"The kids don't need anything, just to see you"

"Okay. I'll bring them a red sox cap"

"If that's what you want to do"

"See you soon, love you"

"Love you too Dad" There was just a hint of anxiety in Maria's voice.

Tony called Jessica "Guess what? I am going to Ohio!"

"Yay!" Jessica had never heard anyone so excited to go to Ohio before.

"I am leaving Thursday and I will be back Monday. Wish me luck"

"You don't need luck. You'll be great"

"Thanks".

It had been so long since Tony went anywhere, he wasn't sure how to do it. He went into the office and Alice helped him make the plane reservations. She even got him an airport limo. Guido paid for the limo as a congratulations present.

Maria was waiting for Tony outside the gate at the airport. "She's beautiful" Tony thought. She did not look any different than the last time he saw her.

"Did you have a nice flight?" she asked

"Yes, it was pleasant. They even gave us a snack"

"Do you have luggage?"

"Just this carry on. I travel light".

Maria drove him to the hotel and got checked in. It was nice little place. Nothing exceptional but clean and quiet. Then they drove to her house. Tony could feel the excitement growing in him as they approached the neighborhood.

"You have been sober?" Maria asked

"Yes" Tony replied, "for a while now"

"I don't want the kids to be hurt, that's why I ask"

"I know, I know" he replied.

Maria lived on a nice ranch house in a neighborhood of small ranches and splits. The yard was well kept. There was a basketball hoop at the edge of the drive way. It was set at eight feet. The boys were still small. The garage door was open, and Tony could see a couple of bicycles hanging on the wall and a workbench across the back. Maria pulled into the garage and shut the car off. They went into the house. Two boys greeted them at the door.

"Luke, Tyler- this is your grandfather" Maria introduced him.

"We know, we know!" they both said, "You showed us his picture". They reached out their hands to shake hands. Tony was holding in a tear when he shook their hands.

"Are you crying grandpa?" Tyler asked.

"It might be just a little dusty in here" Tony replied.

"Come see our room" the boys asked.

They two boys dragged Tony by his hand to their room. It was a chaos of toys and stuffed animals. They showed him their favorite games and their favorite trucks. Tony sat on the floor playing with the trucks with them. He could not have been happier. After about a half hour Maria called in "Boys, time for lunch". She made sandwiches and the four of them sat around the kitchen table. It was one of the better sandwiches Tony had ever had. Maria even had his favorite kind of root beer. The kids had water. Maria did not believe in sugared drinks for them.

"Did you boys have fun with Grandpa? "

"Yes!!!" they both said. "We played trucks. Did you know grandpa knows how to play trucks?"

"No, but I do now. After we eat, I want you boys to go do your reading"

"But Mom, Grandpa is here..."

"He will be here for a few days. you need to do your work."

"They are reading?" Tony asked

"Yes, I have been doing some home schooling to get them a head start when they go to public school"

"Wow, that's great. You have always been smart, that's were they get it I am sure"

"Frank is smart too, just hands on smart" Maria replied.

"Yes, I see that. I didn't always see that, but I have learned"

Tony drank his root beer and looked around the room and off into the distance

"Thank so much for letting me come visit. It means a lot to me" He said to Maria

"It means a lot to me too" Maria was warming up.

While the boys were studying Tony asked of there was anything he could do around the house. He wanted to feel useful.

"The kitchen faucet will not shut all the way off" Maria replied "Frank is good with most things around here, but plumbing is not his favorite"

"Let me look at it" Tony replied. He went on the garage and found some tools. It wasn't hard Frank had his tools perfectly organized. Tony could appreciate that. He shut the water off under the sink and disassembled the faucet. It was a nice faucet. Tony found a gasket with a little tear in it. "This won't be hard to fix' he thought.

"Is there a plumbing supply place nearby? Can I borrow your car?" He asked Maria. She noticed the kitchen faucet in pieces on the counter she could only say yes.

"There is a place right off the highway, we passed it on the way here, about 10 minutes away" She threw him the keys. Tony found the place she told him about pretty easily. It was one of those older supply houses that carried just about anything, but you needed the secret decoder ring to find it. Tony was able to find a guy working there who was just about his age and he thought he would know exactly what to do. Tony held out his hand with the split gasket in it. The guy stared at it for a few seconds and without saying a word walked back behind the counter. About ten minutes passed before he came back out with a little plastic bag in his hand.

"Here you go" He said.

Tony took the bag and examined the contents, there were three little gaskets in there and to his eye they looked like just what he wanted.

"Thanks, I only need one"

"You need three, there are three in there and you might as well replace all three while you have it apart or you will be back here in a month" The plumbing supply guy knew what he was talking about.

"Okay, what do I owe you?"

The plumbing supply guy looked at the little bag and scratched his head for a minute. "A buck fifty"

Tony paid the buck fifty and headed back home. "Can't get service like that at Home Depot" he thought. When he got back to Maria's place Frank was back from work and staring at the disassembled kitchen faucet.

"You can get this back together?" He asked Tony with a little anger in his voice.

"Hi Frank, it's good to see you" Tony held out his hand. Frank took the hand but only held on for a second. "I will have your faucet back together in a few minutes" Tony went back to work. After a while he was done, and he turned the water back on. Frank tried the faucet out.

"This is the best this has worked in a long time, thanks" He was genuinely grateful.

Tony wiped his hands with a rag and started cleaning up the counter and cleaning off the tools he used." You're welcome".

"I can do a lot of things but for some reason I just cannot do plumbing" Frank said.

"I can't operate a Bridgeport to save my life" Tony replied. When Frank and Maria first were married Tony did not fully appreciate the skills Frank had. He thought of him as wrench monkey. A lot has changed in the last few years in Tony's mind. now he knew how skilled Frank's work really was.

"Want to grab a beer and sit out on the porch?" Frank asked.

"You can, I'll have a root beer" Tony replied "I am okay if you want to have a beer though"

Frank grabbed two root beers from the fridge and they went out and sat on the porch. Tony told Frank about the group and Charlie and Bill and Jessica. He told Frank about Lorraine and how funny she was.

"I think I owe you an apology" Tony started to say.

"No, you don't" Frank replied "I may owe you one for doubting you. I can see now you are serious about this"

"You had every right to doubt. The proof is in the fruit as they say. I want to start bearing good fruit. I have spent too much of my time making sour grapes"

"Well I am glad you were able to come out here" Frank seemed genuine.

They had been out there so long it was getting dark.

"You guys coming in? The boys want to say goodnight" Maria called out.

"On our way" Frank said.

The boys came over to Tony and each gave him a bear hug and said goodnight. "See you tomorrow Grandpa?"

"Yup, see you tomorrow boys"

The rest of the visit went by like lightening. Frank took a day off and they made a family trip to an amusement park. Tony rode a roller coaster for the first time in decades. They had cotton candy and fried dough. Tony and Frank talked Maria into suspending some of her strict dietary guidelines for the kids that day. She did so pretty reluctantly but they double teamed her. Maria and Frank took Tony around and shows him all of their favorite places in the area. Tony even got to meet some of Frank's work colleagues. Before he knew it, he was at the airport. The whole family came to see him off.

"Bye grandpa, we are going to miss you come back soon" Both kids clung on to him like vines and would not let go.

"You are welcome back any time" Frank told him. "How about coming for Thanksgiving?"

"Yes Dad, come for thanksgiving- bring Jessica we would love to meet her"

"I will do that. I love you guys"

"We love you to"

The PA called his flight. It was time to board. No one ever boarded a plane with his feet so far off the ground in the history of flying.

CHAPTER 32

EPILOG

Jessica and Tony got married on a warm summer night. Not at the church, not in front of brooding statues of saints or even the art work of the Sunday school kids but at the coffee shop where they first met. Sandy catered. Tom from Pennsylvania was up to play the week end and came to the wedding. Tony pleaded with him and he sang some songs. The guests were very impressed.

"I am sorry I could never figure out how to market your music" Tony said to him.

"I didn't expect you too. No one buys music anymore and especially not from a little guy with a funny guitar"

"But your stuff is art" Tony said

"Not art, not genius, it's just songs. I don't know where they come from, they just are. Is it art? I don't know what art is. All I care is someone comes here and for a couple of hours maybe their day gets better. Maybe one song touches them deep in their soul. Maybe that's art"

"Maybe it is, maybe it is" Tony replied.

Guido was at the wedding. He was the best man and he bought Jessica and Tony a nice vacation to Bermuda. Real Estate was good to Guido.

"Guido, I owe you big time. You hired me when I was wet behind the ears, you put up with me when I turned into a jerk and you got me started on a new life. I read somewhere that you meet angels in your life when you need them most. Maybe you're an angel" Tony was getting sentimental.

"You owe me squat, you would do the same for me. Have safe trip and come back ready to work. Not work hard though I forbid you to ignore your bride."

"I learn that lesson a while ago" Tony replied.

"Hey meat head" It was Lorraine, it may be the first time Tony ever saw Lorraine any where but at her trailer. "Congratulations"

"Thank you, Lorraine,"

"Don't screw this up"

"I will try my best"

"You will DO your best" she replied.

"Yes ma'am" was all Tony dared say.

Maria came up to Tony. The kids and Frank were right behind her. She gave him a big hug and kissed his cheek. The two kids came over and wrapped their arms around his leg. Frank patted him on the back.

"We are so happy for you Dad. Jessica is a great woman. You have earned some happiness."

"Thanks honey, I appreciate it. I am so glad that you could come and so happy the we are able to connect. I missed so much of you growing up and I don't want to miss any more"

They hugged an cried a little and hugged some more.

"Love you dad" Maria said in a quiet voice, barely audible but Tony heard it like a siren.

"Love you too"

Tony and Jessica enjoyed their time in Bermuda. Tony had never been there. They came back and moved in together in a new place. It would be their place.

Tony took one last trip to the trailer. He sold it to some friend of Danny who was getting divorced. As he fumbled with the key unlocking the door a familiar voice shouted.

"Are you okay out there?"

"I'm fine, just fighting this darn door". "For the last time" he thought.

"When's the new guy moving in?"

"I am not sure, Tuesday?"

"I hope he doesn't play that girly bar music loud like you did'

"You'll miss it Lorraine. You'll miss it"

"Yeah, Maybe I will" Tony had gotten used to that gravely voice. Maybe he would miss that too.

It was clouding up. Maybe this night was going to be dark and stormy. Maybe not. Tony was thankful that it wouldn't be a rum and coke night either. He waved to Lorraine and drove off, the sounds of Ray Charles and BB King singing "The Sinner's Prayer" came from his car stereo. When he got home, Jessica greeted him with a kiss. They sat together on their new couch. There sunset outside the window painted the sky from yellow to orange. Jessica handed Tony his guitar. He gave her a puzzled look. "Play me something sweet" she said. He sat down and played her "I'll be here in the morning"

"There's no stronger wind than one that blows down a lonesome railroad line

no prettier sight than looking back on a town you left behind

There's nothing that's as real as love that's in my mind

so close your eyes I'll be here in the morning" (Townes van Zandt)

She smiled.

#end#

16193883R00118

Made in the USA
Middletown, DE
22 November 2018